It all started out as a dare.

"Come on, Sarah. What have you got to lose? Except fun," Maggie added. "Give it a shot. Try something exciting for once. Don't you have the guts?"

"I have as much courage as you do. Pardon me, guts," Sarah amended.

"And that's another thing. Watch your vocabulary. Nothing turns a man off quicker than an intelligent woman."

"Now, that's one point on which we agree," Sarah said. "The minute a man learns I'm a doctor, he's intimidated." Past experience had taught her that. "I've had men actually step back from me."

"Well, there you are," Maggie said. "Ask the guy out, but don't tell him you're a doctor."

"You don't understand. I don't need a man in my life. I'm quite content the way I am. I'm proud of my profession, I've worked hard to get where I am, and I won't be defined by my relationship with a man."

VEDA BOYD JONES writes romances "that confirm my own values," including the award-winning *Callie's Mountain*. Besides her fiction writing, Veda has authored numerous articles for popular periodicals. A sought-after speaker at writers' conferences, Veda lives with her husband, an architect, and three sons in the Ozarks of Missouri.

Books by Veda Boyd Jones

HEARTSONG PRESENTS
HP21—Gentle Persuasion
HP34—Under a Texas Sky
HP46—The Governor's Daughter
HP78—A Sign of Love
HP110—Callie's Mountain
HP154—Callie's Challenge

A Question of Balance

Veda Boyd Jones

Heartsong Presents

Dedication

For my brothers, Michael, Secil, and Stan, with love.

Acknowledgment

Thanks to Dr. Dian Doody, Elaine Jones, Bonnie Hinman, and Joan Banks for their advice on this book. And thanks to Jimmie, Landon, Morgan, and Marshall, who explored Kansas City with me.

A note from the Author:

I love to hear from my readers! You may write to me at the following address:

Veda Boyd Jones
Author Relations
P.O. Box 719
Uhrichsville, OH 44683

ISBN 1-57748-026-0

A QUESTION OF BALANCE

Cover illustration by Brian Bowman.

PRINTED IN THE U.S.A.

one

"Do you think they're laughing at our expense?" Sarah Madison asked her two friends and nodded across the plush restaurant at the table of three men who kept looking their direction.

"Of course they are," Maggie answered, giving her auburn locks a pert shake. "Not us, specifically, but women in general," she was quick to add. "If you'd arrived on time, you'd have seen how they've been giving us the eye all evening. Men are so obvious. I think the one in the blue blazer is interested in me."

"Maggie, you think every man over eighteen is interested in you," Ellen piped in.

Maggie gave a sly smile. "When you've got it, you've got it."

"What is *it*?" Sarah asked.

"If you have to ask, you don't have it," Maggie said and chuckled.

"I think I'm glad I don't," Sarah said. "I apologize again for being late. We're swamped at the hospital." She lifted her glass toward Ellen in a toast. "To the Fabulous Five and to the birthday gal."

The three women clinked their glasses. The pact they had made in high school to celebrate each other's birthday continued even though Mary Lynn in Denver and Connie in Des Moines were missing the dinner.

"The first of the Fab Five to hit thirty," Maggie said. "How does it feel, old-timer?"

"Just like it did yesterday," Ellen said. "I'm consoled by the fact that you'll all be joining me soon."

Sarah smiled at the two women she had known practically all her life. In high school they had been inseparable. They had attended the same youth group at church and had remained close through the years.

Of the Fab Five, Sarah was the only one who had never married. During college she had dated Jeff, but he had objected when she started medical school. The last time she had seen him, he had told her he wanted a beautiful woman like her, but not a woman who would make more money than he did.

Then three years ago, she had dated Troy for several months. When he broke up with her, he had said she gave too much of herself to her patients and not enough to him.

Since that time she had been very careful to avoid an entanglement and she was determined not to be hurt again by men who could not accept her career. She kept relationships on a friendly basis, devoted her energy to her career, and the years had slipped by. Now at twenty-nine years of age, she held an important position at the research hospital working with Dr. Warner Lewis, a renowned physician. She worked with children suffering with leukemia and she found it to be rewarding but emotionally draining; she did not have anything left in her to deal with the fragile egos of men.

Oh, she went to the occasional hospital function with a date, but those were social gatherings she had to attend, and other doctors, usually Hal, escorted her. Yes, she was content in her world, knowing she was making a difference in children's lives but sometimes she could not do enough. Right now she was losing Andrea, one of her little patients and, unless a miracle occurred, Andrea would be the next leukemia victim at the hospital, probably before the week was out.

The three women ordered dinner and settled back to catch up on news. Sarah was glad to be with such comfortable companions after a stress-filled day at the hospital and she forced herself to concentrate on the conversation around her. Sarah had never been good at separating her professional duties from what little personal time she had when the lives of children hung in the balance. She needed tonight and the lighthearted fun of a birthday celebration.

"You know, Sarah, you're missing something by not having *it.*"

Ah, the mysterious *it* again. "Why, Maggie?"

"Well, before you got here, Ellen and I were discussing how serious you are these days. You need some fun in your life. Some romance. . .adventure."

Sarah turned to Ellen, who was nodding her agreement.

"You could have it all, Sarah. You're beautiful and smart, but you spend too much time at that oppressive hospital. When was the last time you laughed?" Ellen asked.

Of all the women in the Fab Five, Sarah felt closest to Ellen who was almost as determined a woman as Sarah thought herself to be. Ellen set her goals and went after them.

The two friends had quarreled only once—five years ago before Ellen's marriage into Kansas City's high society. Kent, the owner and CEO of a computer software company, was twelve years older than Ellen. Sarah had thought them an odd match and asked Ellen if Kent's wealth was part of his attraction. Ellen admitted the money was an added draw and that she wanted the luxuries it could afford her, but she said she loved Kent. Sarah, though, had accused her of being bought.

"Everyone has a price," Ellen had replied.

They had made up, apologized for words that should have never been spoken, and Sarah had been her maid of honor. She was happy to admit she had been wrong. The five-year-old marriage had kept a glow in Ellen's eyes.

Maggie was the most adventurous of the Fab Five. Sarah had always admired Maggie's free spirit and wanted to be more like her. After high school, Maggie had taken off for New York to pursue a career in fashion design. She never made the big time, although she had studied under one of the best designers in the Big Apple. Unfortunately, a brief marriage had changed a happy-go-lucky Maggie into a cynical woman.

"So, you two had a little discussion about my lack of excitement and romance while I wasn't here to defend myself." Sarah did not like the determined glint in Ellen's eyes and could tell that Ellen was up to something.

"You need to get out more. Enjoy life. Have fun," Maggie said.

"I get out," Sarah said. "I just haven't met Mr. Right yet." And she was not looking for him, either for he was a fantasy, like Superman, and did not really exist.

"You'll never meet him if you don't get out of that hospital more often," Ellen said. "You need more balance in your life. Physically you keep in shape; spiritually you have a strong belief in God; intellectually you remain challenged and work toward lofty goals. Emotionally, though, you fall down."

That must have been some discussion they had had. "Do I deserve this just because I was late?" she asked.

Another burst of laughter erupted from the table of men. Three members of the Fab Five glanced across the restaurant.

❧

"Another woman's joined them." Ed motioned with his head as he picked up a hot roll from the basket with one hand and a knife with the other. "Pass the butter, Marshall." He buttered his roll while staring at the women, then dropped his knife, which clattered loudly as it hit the edge of his plate.

"I hope you're more competent with a scalpel than you are with that butter knife," Marshall Adams said. "And why all the interest?I thought you said you were a happily married man."

"I am, I am," Ed said. "But I'm still breathing."

"Not for long if you don't drop some of that extra weight," Jason chimed in and adjusted his blue blazer. He gave the redheaded woman an interested look and a wink. "How much have you put on since medical school, Ed? Fifty pounds? Who's your doctor, anyway? Hasn't he told you how unhealthy all that extra weight is?" Jason nonchalantly tapped a cigarette on the table before he put it to his lips and lit it. He inhaled with a satisfied smile.

"Look who's talking," Ed retorted, waving the smoke out of his way.

"Doctors, doctors," Marshall chided. He really wanted to say, "Boys, boys," but knew they would object. He had been the peacemaker between these two all those years ago in medical school, and his role had not changed with this meeting at the medical convention.

Marshall had been looking forward to this week in Kansas City and to seeing his old friends. The small town where he practiced was exactly where he wanted to be, but he missed the excitement of a city and the anonymity it gave him. Because of his profession, women in his home town vied for his attention. In his younger days he had enjoyed it, but now he was tired of the game. At thirty-four, he wanted to find that special woman, attractive, intelligent, honest, and true, and he wanted to do the chasing.

At least he had never deluded himself about why most women were interested in him now that he was a physician. He was more realistic than Jason. Marshall had helped him through two divorces and understood that Jason's wolfish attitude toward women was a coverup for the hurt and shattered ego he had suffered at the hands of two unscrupulous women who had wanted to be married to a doctor.

Marshall also understood Ed's obsession with food. During their college days, when most medical students had time only for their studies, Ed had held down not one, but two part-time jobs, and still sometimes had gone hungry. Now his financial position had changed and for all his appearance and sometimes rough manner, Ed was a brilliant surgeon. The money poured in, and Ed indulged his weakness for food. He was not as obese as Jason had implied, but he could stand to lose thirty pounds.

"I think the redhead's interested in me," Jason said. "She keeps glancing over here."

Marshall's gaze traveled across twenty feet of deep burgundy carpeting to the table occupied by the three women.

"There's a lot of gold flashing over there. I think at least one of them is married. And you may be right about the redhead, Jase. Women these days sure take the guesswork out of relationships."

"What do you mean?" Ed asked.

"They leave no doubt about what they want—money."

"And social status," Jason added.

"Are you speaking from personal experience?" Ed questioned, his eyebrows raised.

"Actually two experiences," Jason admitted with a

frown. "But Marshall, don't you attribute any of the female pursuit to the famous Adams charm and good looks? Remember how women used to swarm around him in school, Ed?"

"Sure. Never could figure out what his attraction was."

"Wait a minute. Basically I'm a pretty nice guy. That's all it takes. Just a good, all-around personality."

"Uh-huh. Every girlfriend I ever had and both my wives said you had rugged good looks. I never could see it," Jason said.

Marshall shrugged. He glanced at the table of women again. "Yes, Jase, I do believe the redhead is interested in you." He switched the topic away from himself.

"How about that. And she doesn't even know I'm a doctor," Jason said.

Marshall nodded and studied the woman who had joined the other two. She was a stunning blond, a real knockout. When she had entered the restaurant, he had watched her walk gracefully to her table. Her long golden hair was pulled back from her face and was secured by a metal clasp; the suit she wore gave her an air of authority but also flattered her feminine shape. After she exchanged words with the others, she cast a wilting glance at the men.

"Wow. Feel the cold air from the glacier," Jason said. "I wonder if the famous Adams charm could melt her."

"Yeah, Marshall. I don't think she'd pursue you because you're a doctor." Ed laughed out loud, and all three female heads turned toward their table.

❧

"What you need, Sarah, is something out of the ordinary. I'd say you've never even asked a man out," Maggie said.

"You're right," Sarah answered, wondering where this conversation was leading. Her friends were looking her over in a very curious manner.

"It's not that hard," Maggie said. "Men love it when women show a little initiative."

"Have you taken a survey?" Sarah asked dryly.

"Personal experience. Let's face it, men can be easily manipulated. If a woman shows a man a little interest, he's down on his knees, just waiting for the leash to be put around his neck. Even you could do it."

Sarah's fork stopped halfway to her mouth. "Even me?"

"Let's face it. You're a novice at this sort of thing. But I have a little proposition. Check out the one in the tweed jacket. I dare you to ask him out."

At the word *dare,* Sarah's eyebrows shot up. In their younger days she and Maggie had dared each other to do a number of things that usually ended up getting them in trouble. But it had been years since they had been caught wading in the big fountain at the Plaza Shopping Center, the last of many dares.

Maggie waved a finger at Sarah. "If you played your cards right, you could convince that guy to go anywhere you wanted. Say to the fashion show Saturday." The clothing store where she worked as fashion coordinator was giving a benefit fashion show for Sarah's hospital. "What do you say?"

"I say you're out of your mind."

"Come on, Sarah. What have you got to lose? Except fun," Maggie added. "Give it a shot. Try something exciting for once. Don't you have the guts?"

"I have as much courage as you do. Pardon me, guts," Sarah amended.

"And that's another thing. Watch your vocabulary. Nothing turns a man off quicker than an intelligent woman."

"Now, that's one point on which we agree," Sarah said. "The minute a man learns I'm a doctor, he's intimidated." Past experience had taught her that. "I've had men actually step back from me."

"Well, there you are," Maggie said. "Ask the guy out, but don't tell him you're a doctor."

"You don't understand. I don't need a man in my life. I'm quite content the way I am. I'm proud of my profession, I've worked hard to get where I am, and I won't be defined by my relationship with a man."

"I think you protest too much," Maggie said. "Are you afraid of men, Sarah?"

Sarah took in a quick breath and glanced at Ellen, who sat intently watching the exchange. "I'm not afraid of men. I deal with them every day." This conversation had gone on long enough. She would put Maggie on the defensive. "What would be more interesting would be for you to get the man in the blue blazer to go out with you. And you can't do the asking. I dare you to get him to the fashion show."

"No problem," Maggie said. "I prefer the direct approach, but I could get him to do the asking. I'll accept the dare if you will."

"This is ridiculous," Sarah said and shook her head.

"Maybe not," Ellen said. "It might do you both good. Prove that you have different sides to your personalities than we normally see."

"Come on, Sarah. It'll be fun," Maggie coaxed. "For once you could play a dumb blond."

Not for once, but for the third time, Sarah thought as Jeff and Troy flitted through her mind. She had learned the hard way that some men preferred airheads to smart women.

"No," she said with finality in her voice. "He could be married."

"I don't see a ring," Ellen said. "And of course, if he is married, we'll call the whole thing off."

"No," Sarah repeated. "Nothing would make me take this dare."

"Oh, really? What if there were a sizable incentive?" Ellen asked.

"I can't be bought," Sarah said, then regretted her choice of words.

"Let's talk about fifty-thousand dollars to be awarded not just to your hospital, but to your clinical research."

Sarah's mouth flew open.

"Kent just told me I needed to divest us of fifty-thousand dollars. . .to charity." She studied her nails for a moment. "He doesn't care where our charitable contributions go; that's one of my jobs. I could funnel it all to leukemia research at Children's Research Hospital and hand you the check at the fashion show Saturday." She flashed a quick, catbird smile.

Sarah closed her mouth but remained speechless. Fifty-thousand dollars could mean a great deal to her lab and might save the lives of countless children. It was too late for little Andrea, but if they could find another way of combating the cancer, it might give hope for other little girls like her. They had received a research grant last year, but this year little money had trickled down from the administration. Ellen and Kent donated thousands to charity every year, and it might as well be to further leukemia research.

"But you can't tell him you're a doctor," Maggie said.

"I would never lie," Sarah said. That went against her values.

"Well, telling a guy you're a doctor is like the kiss of death to romance. You said so yourself," Maggie said. "You need to get away from the doctor/lawyer professional type of relationship. You need a man/woman relationship. If he asks where you work, say you teach health. You do teach interns, don't you?"

"That's a technicality, and you know it." She lectured interns when they went through the pediatric oncology rotation. "Besides, I can't act like what I'm not." Sarah shook her head. Was she actually considering such a crazy idea?

"Just don't act like what you are," Maggie said.

Sarah glanced over at the man in the tweed jacket. His wavy, dark hair gleamed when it caught the light of the chandelier. His good looks were of the rugged type. Even sitting down, he positively radiated power. Maybe it was the broad shoulders. She frowned at him as she considered the dare. Could her friends be right? Was she too serious and leading an unbalanced life? All work and no play and all that?

What harm could possibly come of the dare? It would be a temporary setup, so it would not disturb her neatly ordered life. This was Monday; Saturday was only five days away. It might be a way of proving to Ellen that she did not need help with her love life. Ellen never called them blind dates, but on several occasions when Sarah had gone to dinner at Ellen and Kent's, she had discovered an extra man at the table.

"To keep the numbers even," Ellen had always said.

There was also the fifty-thousand dollars, an enormous amount for a private donation. Actually, that was the only reason she would do it. Research cost money, and every dollar could make a difference.

She glanced at the man again. He caught her eye and smiled at her, a warm, gentle smile. Against her will, she felt the corners of her lips curve up in an answering gesture.

It felt odd, and she could not remember the last time she had smiled at a man like that.

"All right," she told her friends. "I'll do it."

❧

"Did you see that, Ed?" Jason asked. "She smiled at him. I knew the old Adams charm was still there." He slapped his hand on the table. "And you always get the classiest ones. How do you do it?"

"All I did was smile."

"Hey, maybe the glacier's the one," Ed said. "See if she'll go out with you before you tell her you're a doctor."

"Yeah," Jason agreed. "If the glacier will go out with you, you'll know you still have the Adams charm."

"I could do it, but I don't want to." Marshall had come here to update his skills and to renew his friendship with these men, not to get involved with a woman. Besides, a man could not ask a woman he saw across a restaurant for a date. And he did not want to be shot down in front of these men.

"You don't want to meet the classiest looking woman in the place?" Jason asked. "What happened to the old Marshall Adams?"

Maybe Marshall could convince this woman to see him, to just have a cup of coffee with him. There was something about her that intrigued him. He glanced over at the woman and smiled.

Again she returned his smile, and the expression on her face softened.

"All right. I'll give it a try," said Marshall.

❧

Sarah finished her cheesecake and laid down her fork. What had she gotten herself into? She had no idea of how to ask a man out. After all, he was sitting with two other men. Did she confront him with them listening?

The three women had gone over the ground rules of the dare: Have fun, don't tell him you're a doctor, and get him to the fashion show on Saturday. Maggie had agreed to her dare, too.

"I know you won't donate money to my bank account," she had said, "but it'll be fun. And if it will get Sarah out, I'm willing to make the sacrifice."

Sure, thought Sarah. Since Maggie was between relationships, it would also give her a man to date for a week. The blond man looked interested enough; Sarah had seen him wink at Maggie.

"They're already on dessert," Ellen whispered conspiratorially. "You're going to have to make your move soon. What are you going to do, Sarah?"

"I'm not sure. Maggie?"

"You go first, Sarah, since you need the experience. Pretend you're a siren. You can do it."

"Thanks." Her friends stared at her, waiting. Taking a deep breath, Sarah stood, smoothed down the skirt of her rust-colored suit, and straightened her jacket. She placed some bills on the table to take care of her check, hooked the strap of her purse over her shoulder, and walked purposefully toward the table of men. She could do this. She was a woman of the nineties.

Each step shortened the expanse of burgundy carpeting between the tables. She could feel the eyes of the women on her back and those of the men on her face. Suddenly, she could not do it. She veered off her straight course, headed for the door, and slipped out into the foyer. Perhaps they would all believe she had gone to the ladies' room.

She leaned against the wall and closed her eyes. For the kind of money Ellen was offering, surely she could go back in there and talk to the man.

"Dear God, please give me the courage to do this," she whispered.

At the sound of the door opening, she opened her eyes and straightened up. Her victim stood in front of her.

"Hi," he said and smiled that charming smile of his.

"Hello," Sarah replied in what she hoped was a flirty tone. Was she that out of practice that she had forgotten how to flirt? This was her opportunity, but she felt as tongue-tied as a shy teenager. "Did you enjoy your dinner?" What a silly thing to say.

"Yes, I did. And now I'd like a cup of coffee. Would you join me?" He motioned to another room off the foyer that housed the Java Room.

"Yes, I'd like that," she said, then she actually giggled in relief. She had not giggled in years; she had not even laughed lately. Maybe her friends were right. Maybe she did need more fun in her life, more balance.

"I need to tell my friends to leave without me," she said. "I'll just be a minute."

He held the door open, and the couple walked back into the restaurant. Sarah walked quickly to the table where Ellen and Maggie waited, wide-eyed.

"We're going for coffee," she announced in a low voice.

"All right!" Maggie said. "I thought you'd chickened out on us."

"Oh, please," Sarah said. She was not about to reveal that he had asked her. "See you later."

"I'll call you tomorrow," Ellen said as Sarah turned and

walked back to where Marshall stood by his table. The other men grinned at her, but Marshall escorted her out of the restaurant without a backward glance at his friends.

He kept a guiding hand on her back as they crossed the foyer and entered the espresso bar. Unlike the old brightly lit, counter-type coffee shops of the past, the Java Room was lit almost entirely by candlelight. From the center of each table, a tall taper glowed. The piano held a brass candelabra and was the only light available for the pianist, a woman in a long, black dress.

"This is lovely," Sarah murmured as she sat in the chair Marshall pulled out for her. "Wow, what a classy place," she said on second thought. Maybe she should watch her language as Maggie had suggested.

Instead of taking the chair opposite her, Marshall sat in a seat at a right angle to her.

Although the room was practically filled, a waitress appeared immediately and presented a long-stemmed rose to Sarah and took their orders.

Sarah glanced around and noticed the other women had roses, too. It was a classy place, she thought.

"So, what's your name?" she asked.

"Marshall Adams from Neosho, Missouri." He hesitated a moment. She had agreed to get a coffee without knowing he was a doctor. Surely that was enough to prove he still had the Adams charm. Now he wanted to know her better, without making up stories or avoiding the truth. "I'm here for the AMA convention. Your turn."

"Sarah Madison. I live here in Kansas City." She extended her hand and he shook it, gently but firmly. "Are you a doctor?"

At his nod, she said, "How interesting. I'm a—" she caught herself just in time. "I teach health."

"Really?" His baritone voice had her hypnotized. Kansas City's an interesting place. I'd like to see some of it while I'm here."

Great. He was walking right into her lair. "Maybe I could show you around." If she entertained him, he would feel he owed her the favor of attending that fashion show, and she would get fifty thousand for research.

"I'd like that," he said and smiled at her.

"So, you're a doctor," she said. "Where did you go to school?" It was small talk she hoped a happy-go-lucky, not-a-care-on-her-mind type of woman would ask.

"University of Chicago," he answered.

"Really? I went there," she said. "Did you have Strausburg for basic anatomy?" Now why did she ask that? She should steer him away from talk of college. But didn't health majors take anatomy? Maybe he would let that slip by.

"Yes, I did. He's an institution in himself. When were you there?"

They discovered that Sarah was a freshman when he was an intern.

"In the same university and I didn't know it. Of course, you'd have been in the education school, so our paths wouldn't have crossed. But now my luck has changed." It sounded like a line, but he meant it.

"Sarah?"

Sarah turned her head to see Hal standing beside their table. He was an occasional date, but she knew he was not the fantasy Mr. Right.

Oh, no, she thought. *He could ruin everything.*

"Hello, Hal." This restaurant and coffee bar was within a block of the convention hotel. She figured that was why Marshall and his cronies had dined there and why Hal was there now.

Hal stared pointedly at Marshall.

"Hal, this is Dr. Marshall Adams from Neosho. He's here for the convention. Marshall, Dr. Harold Mosley from Children's Research Hospital." She gave his full name and added, "He specializes in cardiology."

The two men shook hands and exchanged civilities, but eyed each other with great interest.

"Have you known Sarah long?" Hal asked.

"We both went to the University of Chicago," Marshall answered.

"Ah, old friends. I see. Sarah and I also go back quite a ways. At Children's Research—"

Sarah felt the money for the research slipping away.

two

"Hal," Sarah interrupted, "are you with those doctors? I think they're leaving." She pointed to several men who had walked up behind him.

"Yes, but I can join—"

"Actually," she said, "I wanted to spend some time with Marshall. Catch up on old times, you understand?" Why wouldn't he go away? She had been downright rude.

Hal glanced behind him then back at Sarah and Marshall. "I guess I'd better go," he said. "I'll talk to you tomorrow."

"Fine," Sarah said, but she did not take a deep breath until he and the other doctors had left. Another doctor from Children's Research was with his group, and she had been afraid he would mention something about her work, too.

She glanced at Marshall and saw he was watching her. "Sorry. He's someone I've dated now and again, but I'm not interested, and he can't get the message." She had told her friends she would not lie, and here she was telling a whopper. Or was she? On quick reflection, Sarah knew it was true. She liked Hal as a friend, enjoyed the evenings he took her to hospital functions, but he seemed determined to turn their relationship into more than a casual friendship.

Marshall nodded and held up his cup. "To Kansas City," he said as he clinked his cup with hers.

"To Neosho," she said. "Right?"

"Yes. My hometown."

"You're from there originally?"

He nodded. "When I was a youngster, I wanted desperately to get out of Neosho and move to a big city. But after medical school, when I was deciding where I wanted to practice, I decided on a small town. I kept thinking about some place like Neosho and finally thought, why not go home?"

"What happened to 'You can't go home again?' Do you disagree with Thomas Wolfe?" Oh, no. She had done it again. She should not talk about literature.

"You can go home again, but you go back as a different person and demand to be treated as an adult and not as a child. Of course, it helped that I had M.D. after my name."

Sarah nodded in agreement. She had found the same thing was true for her, although she had always wanted to return to Kansas City. She liked cities, but then they were all she had ever known.

"Cities are like many small towns put together. Basically I stay in one small area, maybe three miles square. But if I want to do something different, it's always available just across the city."

"I know. Remember, I lived in Chicago for several years."

"That's right." They discussed the Windy City and its points of interest.

"To think, we were in the same town and didn't know it," he said.

Her heart quickened. What was wrong with her? He was only giving her what sounded like a line. But it was a sign that he was interested. Time to turn on the charm. What did women say in a situation like this?

"What's your sign?" she said then smiled brightly. She

felt foolish saying it, but it was part of the game.

"My sign?" Marshall asked. He looked at her oddly, as if trying to see behind her mind.

His eyes were the bluest she had ever seen. They would make Mel Gibson's look pale. Even in the flickering candlelight, their color was brilliant.

"Your astrological sign," Sarah explained.

Marshall studied her for a brief moment. She was sending him mixed messages. When he had first seen her in the restaurant, she had given all three men a look that would have wilted lettuce, as if she were disgusted with the whole male/female game. Yet, without the slightest hesitation, and almost eagerly, she had accepted his suggestion that they go for coffee. She was an educated woman, had read Thomas Wolfe, but was also interested in astrological small talk.

"I'm a Pisces. Do you believe that stuff?" Marshall asked.

She looked directly in his eyes. "No," she said softly. She had vowed she would not lie, and she wouldn't, at least not directly.

"Then why discuss it?"

What could she say? That she was so out of practice at flirting that she did not know how to make small talk with a man? No, he would ask why she was out of practice and that would lead to her job and then to disclosing the dare, and that she could not do.

"I'm getting mixed signs from you, Sarah Madison. And I don't mean the astrological kind. I think you're an intelligent woman with whom I would like to spend some time, and then I get a flash of dumb blond. Which is it?"

Sarah's mouth dropped open. "You don't like dumb blonds?"

Marshall shook his head "no," his gaze never leaving hers.

"Men don't like intelligent women," she said.

"Now who would tell you something like that? Surely not a man."

Surely one would, she thought, *actually two*. But she did not say it out loud. Jeff had not only said it, his actions had shouted it. Troy had been a little more discreet, but his message had been clear enough.

"Actually we were discussing men at dinner, and it came up." She leaned toward him to get a closer look at his expression. "Are you sure you'd prefer an intelligent woman?"

"Any day of the year. And especially this day."

Sarah smiled. This was a man who could appreciate her for herself. And she wanted to get to know him, not on a professional level, but as a woman knows a man. Surely she could do that without revealing she was a doctor. The dare was important. She hated to admit that she could be bought, but she reminded herself the money was not for her, but for the children. There was also the competition with Maggie over who could get a man to the fashion show. Although she did not think of herself as competitive, she knew she had to be in order to make it as far as she had in a male-dominated profession.

The medical convention ended on Saturday night with the banquet. The closing speaker was none other than her boss, Dr. Warner Lewis, and she already had a ticket for the event. Right after the fashion show she would tell Marshall about the dare, and they would laugh about it, and he would tell her how smart she was to get that much money for her research. Then they would attend the banquet together, and after that go their separate ways. No involvement, no dependency, but a good time for a week. That was exactly the way she wanted it.

Yes, she wanted to know this man, and she wanted him to know her, her real self. The self who liked sunrises and pralines and ice cream. The one who gained serenity and peace from early morning church services and cried over late night movies. The self that she rarely showed to the world. She would share that self with him, all except the part about being a doctor. Then he would go back to his small town, she would stay in her city, and they would have enjoyed a pleasant interlude.

"Marshall, may we join you?" Jason, Marshall's friend from dinner was standing by their table with a triumphant Maggie at his side.

Marshall stood. He did not want Jason and the redhead to sit with them, but a quick glance around the full room convinced him he had no choice. "Of course," he conceded. As soon as the redhead sat down, Marshall resumed his seat and cast an apologetic look at Sarah. Things were just getting interesting, and now he could feel Sarah withdrawing.

After introductions and more coffee and a rose, Maggie dominated the conversation. "Marshall, did Sarah tell you she teaches health?" she asked.

"Yes, she did," he said and wondered briefly why Maggie was interested in their conversation. "What do you do for a living, Maggie?"

"I'm a fashion coordinator for Ambassadors, a big department store chain." She sipped her chocolate latte. Hmm, this is good." In the silence, she elaborated. "I do fashion shows a lot. General PR stuff, too. I'm doing a fashion show at Sarah's hospital Saturday."

"You own a hospital, Sarah?" Jason asked.

"No, of course not. Maggie calls Children's Research Hospital mine because I work a lot of hours there without getting paid," Sarah explained, shooting daggers at Maggie for her slip. She figured she put in many unpaid hours.

"Oh, you're a volunteer?" Jason asked, but Sarah did not answer. "Hospitals couldn't operate without them. We call them Pink Ladies at Denver General."

"Doctors, would you excuse us a moment while we visit the powder room?" Sarah asked, then practically dragged Maggie off with her.

"What's the big deal, Maggie?" She accosted her as soon as they were in the ladies' room. "Why did you say my hospital?"

Maggie shrugged. "It slipped out. Sorry."

"I want that money for research, so don't mess this up. If it weren't for you, I might have persuaded Ellen to donate it without the dare. Now I have to be on my toes all the time with Marshall. He's a nice man, and I'd like to get to know him better."

"Ah-hah! You'd have never asked him out without the dare, so you owe me one," Maggie said. "Besides, Saturday's not that far away. You can tell him as soon as the check's in your hand." She looked a little sheepish and admitted,

"Actually, Jason's a real nice guy. Too bad he leaves Sunday for Denver, but maybe he'll ask me out there soon."

Sarah gave her a disbelieving look.

"He might," Maggie argued, her voice going up an octave. "Forget about Jason and me. You concentrate on Marshall. He'll be glad you didn't talk shop the whole time. Trust me." She turned and led the way back to the men.

Maggie could have a point. Marshall might say he did not like dumb blonds, but he might not like women doctors, either. Some male doctors were threatened by them.

"Oh, Maggie," Sarah said before they were within hearing range of the doctors, "how did you manage to be here with Jason?"

"I accidently bumped into him in the foyer. We started talking, and he suggested coffee. I wanted to be more original than that, but it worked." She shrugged her shoulders again, a habit that was beginning to annoy Sarah.

The two men were deep in conversation and looked up guiltily as the two women approached the table. Sarah exchanged a curious look with Maggie. The men stood as the women were seated, then resumed their own chairs.

An uncomfortable silence followed. The pianist had taken a break and conversations from the other tables could be heard.

"There seem to be a lot of doctors here," Maggie said. "Is it a big convention?"

"Several thousand," Jason answered. "We were lucky to get rooms in the convention hotel. We can walk to the Convention Center for the big meetings and just go downstairs for the smaller seminars. Marshall and I were just discussing what a nice diversion it is to have two lovely women with us instead of hearing shoptalk all night as well as at the meetings."

Maggie shot Sarah an I-told-you-so look. "Well, we'll see what else we can do to keep you away from all these doctors."

"Marshall, you mentioned you wanted to see some of Kansas City," Sarah said. "Anything special?"

"You tell me. The few times I've been here were for specific events with no extra time for exploring the area.

When we go to a city from Neosho, we head for Tulsa. It's closer."

"Are you a baseball fan? The Royals are in the play-offs, and tomorrow night they play here again. If they win, they'll go to the World Series."

"I love baseball." Marshall's eyes sparkled with excitement. "I've always been a Cardinals fan, but I can switch loyalties for one night. Can we get tickets this late?"

"Tickets aren't a problem. My family has a box. It's my dad's one great passion, but he and Mom are in Connecticut visiting my sister, who just made me an aunt for the third time. So, the box is mine." She was glad he liked baseball. Getting him into this special play-off game should make him feel indebted enough to attend the fashion show with her.

"Marshall obviously hasn't told you about the big game against the Goodman town team," Jason said. He lowered his voice to imitate an announcer. "He was eighteen and playing for the American Legion team. Top of the ninth, bases loaded, score one-oh in favor of the Neosho team, when Goodman's big slugger came up to bat. You may have guessed that the southpaw on the mound was none other than Marshall Adams."

Marshall groaned. "I was going to impress her with that old story when we were alone."

"Go ahead. Impress me now," Sarah said.

"Ah, it was nothing," Marshall said with false modesty. "Just three pitches and three strikes and we won the game, the league, and the trophy."

"But how did the runners get on base in the first place?" Sarah asked, effectively puncturing his balloon.

"Well, I can't remember exactly. Maybe a walk and a couple of hits. That's not the important part, Sarah," he said in an exaggerated gruff voice.

Maggie burst out laughing and Jason joined in. Sarah maintained a straight face. "You're right, of course, Marshall. Let me feel your muscle." She reached over and massaged his left bicep through his tweed jacket. "You're strong. It must take a lot of strength to throw the ball that hard," she said in a sultry voice.

Marshall leaned over and whispered in her ear. "Forget what I said earlier. I might get to like the dumb blond routine."

He was kidding, of course, Sarah thought. But as she looked into his eyes, she saw interest mixed with humor. He took her hand and held it. With his touch, her heart skipped a beat but her mind recorded his reaction to her dumb blond comment as something to think about later.

While the conversation continued around them, he held her hand, sometimes in one hand, sometimes with both hands. She hated to admit it, but she liked it very much. It was a simple gesture, not a threatening one, but she was tingling down to the tips of her toes.

"I'm sorry to break this up," she said after they had finished their coffees, "but unlike some, who can sleep until meeting time rolls around and then skip if they want, I have to be at work early tomorrow." She stood and Marshall stood with her. He was very tall. She was five foot eight and she only came to his shoulder.

"What about the game tomorrow night?" Jason asked.

"Meet at my place, and we'll go from there. Maggie can direct you. Six-thirty." She waved a good-bye.

Marshall put his arm around her shoulders as they walked out of the candlelit room into the bright foyer. Sarah carried the long-stemmed rose the waitress had given her.

"I do love the smell of roses," she said as she sniffed it, then held it under Marshall's nose.

"Mmm. It smells lovely," he agreed.

They stepped outside into a perfect September evening. The moon was almost full, and the air held a cool hint of fall.

"Did you drive?" he asked.

"My car's in the shop being fixed and won't be ready until tomorrow. I'll take a cab."

"I'll see you home," he said and motioned to a cab parked in a yellow zone. His car was parked a block away at the hotel's underground lot, but this way he could concentrate on Sarah rather than on driving.

"That's not necessary," Sarah protested.

"Don't argue, lady. This way I'll know how to get to your house tomorrow night." He settled himself in the backseat beside her, his arm quite naturally going around her, and her head quite naturally settling on his shoulder.

Sarah straightened and gave the cab driver her address, then once more snuggled close to Marshall. She could not believe she had done that, but admitted to herself that it was where she wanted to be. This dare had somehow freed her. She felt free from responsibility, free from being serious, and free to respond exactly as she wanted to to a good-looking man. She would never see him after Saturday, so would not have a complicated relationship to break.

They were nearing her neighborhood when Marshall gently tilted up her chin and kissed her.

"We're here," the cab driver announced.

Sarah sprang away from Marshall. How could she have let herself be carried away like that? She had let him kiss her with another man a couple of feet away. The cabbie was surely aware of what was going on in the backseat. Feeling free was one thing but acting like the stereotypical dumb blond was something else.

"I'd better go in," she said hastily. She grabbed her purse and waited while Marshall spoke to the driver, opened the door, and climbed out ahead of her.

"Do you think you can find my house tomorrow night?" Sarah asked as they walked to the front door of her Georgian-style home.

"Not at the moment, but I'll watch how the cab takes me to the hotel." He looked up at the massive columns that stretched two stories. "Nice house. You live here alone?"

"Yes. My family lived here when I was younger. When my folks moved out to Lake Quivera, I bought it from them."

"Lake Quivera? A suburb?"

"On the Kansas side. Private community, homes on the golf course, that sort of thing."

Sarah found the key in her purse and opened the front door. Before she could reach in to flick on the light, Marshall put his hands on her shoulders and turned her to face him. Where his kiss in the cab had been tender, questioning, searching, this kiss was assertive, masculine.

Sarah kissed him back, then she pulled away. She had just met the man, and however much she was attracted to him, she was not going to let herself become involved. He would be gone in a few days. Besides, this was their first date, and a pickup date, at that. Worse still, it was a dare. She kept losing sight of that.

"I'll see you tomorrow night. Six-thirty. Game's at eight, but it takes a while to get there and get in. We can grab a hot dog at Kauffman Stadium."

"I'm looking forward to it, Sarah." He gave her a quick

peck on the lips then walked back to the waiting cab.

Marshall climbed onto the backseat and slid toward the center so he could converse easily with the driver and learn the turns he should make to get back to Sarah's. Putting his hand down on the seat next to him, he jerked it back with a little yelp and stuck his injured finger in his mouth. Sarah had left her rose, and his second finger had found a thorn.

He gingerly lifted the flower and sniffed the delicate fragrance. He would never see a rose again without thinking of Sarah. Sarah with the golden hair and the mistaken notion that men did not like intelligent women. She was the kind of woman a man could take home to meet his family.

What was he thinking? He had just met the woman. He was attracted to her, but he did not know her well enough for these serious thoughts. Besides, this had started as an experiment to see if he could get a date with a woman who did not know he was a doctor. And he had succeeded. Getting to know her better and going to a play-off ball game were added bonuses.

When the cab delivered him to the hotel, he took the back stairs to the sixth floor to avoid the milling doctors. Once in his room, he unwrapped a cellophane-covered glass, filled it with water for the rose, and set it on his bedside table.

three

"Marshall, over here," Ed's voice boomed out.

Marshall stopped just inside the door of the large meeting room and looked around until he spotted Ed, waving his big hand in the air. He could see Ed's grin and knew he would be hit with questions about Sarah. Raising his hand in acknowledgment, he took time to speak casually to a few other doctors he had met in other meetings before ambling over to his friend.

"Well? How did it go last night?" Ed's grin got bigger.

"Sarah's quite a woman. We had coffee and a nice chat. We're going to a ball game tonight."

"To the Royals' game? How'd you manage that? If they win tonight, they'll play in the series."

"Sarah has a box for the season," Marshall said, wishing Ed would lower his voice. "Jason and Maggie are going, too."

"Is Maggie the redhead who *accidentally* bumped into Jason last night?"

"Yes." Marshall glanced at his watch—10:30. He had already called the hospital to check on an elderly patient and to make sure the transfer of his caseload to another doctor was going smoothly—10:31. It was going to be a long day before he could meet Sarah at her home.

Sarah. There was something about that woman that fascinated him, although he did not know much about her. He had thought of sending her roses to replace the one he had in his room, but he did not know where she taught health.

Although she hadn't said, he figured she taught in a high school, but he had no idea which one. He gathered she volunteered at Children's Research Hospital, but he did not know which days or which floor, so he dismissed that idea. Tonight he would find out more about her.

He was almost as excited about seeing the ball game as he was about seeing Sarah again. He had never seen a play-off for a World Series game. In Chicago he had ventured to the ballpark a couple of times, but free time had been hard to come by when he was in school, and later, when he was an intern and a resident, free time was nonexistent.

The speaker was counting into the microphone, so Marshall took a seat beside Ed and prepared to take notes on the latest discoveries on how bacteria form in the body.

❧

Sarah sat on the side of the hospital bed admiring Andrea's new doll. This was the fourth time in the last two months that Andrea had been in the hospital and Sarah knew she would not be leaving this time. Acute lymphocytic leukemia, which was once considered fatal, now had a 70 percent recovery rate. But the nonlymphocytic type, which Andrea had, let only 40 percent survive. This little six-year-old girl would be one of the 60 percent.

"Have you named her yet?" Sarah asked.

"I'm going to call her Sarah," Andrea announced proudly.

"Good choice, Andrea. Are you trying to get on my good side?" Sarah teased.

"Which side is your good side, Dr. Sarah?" The frail little girl looked from one side of the doctor to the other, a twinkle in her brave, brown eyes.

Sarah turned her profile for the benefit of her young patient. "This is my better side, you little scamp." She leaned down and hugged Andrea. "I've got to check on a few more patients, then I'll be back." She hung the chart at the foot of Andrea's bed, then called, "I'll see you later," over her shoulder.

Sarah stepped out of the room and took a deep breath. Andrea represented the hardest part of her job. As many times as she had told herself not to get involved with her patients, she always violated that rule and loved each one.

She checked on a couple of other patients, then stopped at the nurses' station to use the phone.

"Arlie, this is Sarah Madison. I'm fine, thanks," she answered. "Arlie, I need a favor. I'm bringing a *real* baseball fan to the game tonight, and I'd appreciate it if you'd meet him after the game."

"Sure," the deep voice answered. "You want the usual . . .an autographed picture and a small tee shirt?"

"No. This one's not a patient. The shirt would have to be extra large."

"A man, Sarah? You're bringing a date to the game?"

"Yes, Arlie. Will you meet him, please?"

"Sure. Is he a doctor?"

"Yes." Sarah twirled the phone cord with her finger and wondered what words to use, then blurted out, "He doesn't know I'm one, too. Be sure not to mention it, okay?"

"What's the deal, Sarah? I thought you always dealt honestly in all relationships. You certainly told me fast enough you weren't interested."

"Now, Arlie. You know we were destined to be just friends. And who's that woman in the picture in yesterday's paper? You two looked pretty chummy."

"We are. I want you to meet Heather. Hey, tonight after the game, I'll have some friends over, and you can meet her then. Bring your date," he added.

"Actually there's another couple doubling with us."

"Safety in numbers, Sarah?"

"Not at all. It just worked out that way," she defended herself. Arlie was too analytical. He thought he had her all figured out.

"Bring them along. The more the merrier and all that."

"Thanks, Arlie. If you need a favor sometime, call on me."

"You can bet I will," Arlie said. "See you tonight."

"See you. And I hope you hit a homer." Sarah hung up the phone with a satisfied smile on her face. Since Marshall liked baseball so much, surely he would like to meet some major league players. He would be so beholden to her, he could not refuse to attend the fashion show. That research money was as good as hers already.

"Dr. Madison," a nurse said, "Mrs. Garren is back from breakfast and is with Andrea. She's sorry she missed you earlier, but would like to speak with you when you have a moment."

"Thanks," Sarah said. "I'll go now and come back in a few minutes to finish rounds." She glanced at her watch. Only 10:40, hours before she would meet Marshall again. But she could not dwell on that now. She squared her shoulders and marched toward Room 202 to talk with the mother of the dying child.

❧

Sarah sat in the front seat of Marshall's luxurious sedan giving him directions while Jason and Maggie shared the backseat.

Marshall had turned the car into her driveway exactly on the stroke of six-thirty. The three were excited and in high spirits about the game and teased Sarah for making them wait five minutes while she changed into jeans.

Sarah had been late getting home. When she realized she would be delayed at the hospital, she called Jefferson Wright, a former patient's father, to make sure she could get into the stadium without having the special play-off tickets. She knew of the drawer at her parents' house where tickets were always kept, but she did not have time for the drive out to Lake Quivera to get them. And she still did not have a car. By the time she left the hospital the garage was closed, so she had taken a cab home.

Jefferson had assured her that he would take care of her. She should find his ticket booth, and he would make sure she got to her box without any hassle, convincing her that it truly was a who-you-know world.

Sarah directed Marshall to the stadium and took ribbing about her last-second instructions, as she would say, "Turn there. . .turn here," when they were almost past the turns.

Marshall pulled the car up outside the gate to Kauffman Stadium.

Jason whistled. "Look at that line."

"That's why we're here an hour before the game," Sarah said. "We have quite a walk from the parking lot before we get to stand in line."

Marshall followed directions from one waving parking attendant to another and finally headed into a space and parked. The foursome trouped to the stadium, joining a throng of people converging at the ticket gates.

"Box seats," Marshall read from a sign. "Over here." He had taken Sarah's hand so they would not be separated in the push of the crowd, and now he pulled her toward that line.

Sarah squinted to see the attendant taking tickets at the front of the line. "No, that's not Jefferson," she said and led them to the next line.

"Who is Jefferson, and why are we looking for him?" Marshall asked.

Sarah explained the situation and kept urging them from line to line. *This can't be happening to me,* she thought, as they checked out the third and fourth lines. With each line they passed, she became more embarrassed.

"Here he is," she called out with relief. It was the sixth ticket booth they had checked, and now they had to go to the end of the long line. Luckily the line moved fast and, within ten minutes, they were talking to Jefferson, who handed Sarah a makeshift pass for four.

"Thanks, Jefferson," she said. "You're a real lifesaver."

"No, you're the real lifesaver. I'll never forget what you did for Nathan."

"He was a good patient," Sarah said, glancing over her shoulder to make sure Marshall had not heard. He and Jason were talking, so she felt safe. "Let's go," she said to her companions.

Marshall again took her hand as they walked into the stadium. Another attendant stopped them to look at the pass and waved them on. After climbing three separate levels of wide ramps, Sarah motioned them to turn left and go into the open air.

The sunlight was just fading, and the lights around the playing field and those in the stands had been turned on. The excitement in the air was contagious as the loud hum from thousands of conversations reached their ears. As if on cue, the loudspeaker began the introductions of the players. The foursome stood in awe for a moment, before Sarah urged them on down the steps toward the box seats. She kept glancing ahead for an empty box while she manipulated them past the people in the aisles. Why couldn't she see one? She checked the ticket again to make sure Jefferson had written the correct section number. He had. She stopped in the right spot and counted over three boxes.

"Oh, no," she gasped.

"What is it?" Marshall asked and grabbed her shoulders. "Are you all right?"

"This can't happen to me," Sarah said in a whisper, but Marshall was right beside her and heard even though the stadium thundered with applause for the players.

"My father's friends are in the box. He must have given them the tickets since he couldn't use them."

She watched disappointment wash over Marshall's face then saw it quickly replaced by a forced smile.

"Well, we can always go to a movie," he suggested.

"No. Let's find Jefferson." She did not know what he could do, the game was a sellout, but she needed to make some effort to get herself out of this mess. She closed her eyes briefly to gain her composure.

"What's going on?" Maggie asked as Sarah turned to lead them back up the steps to the platform where they had entered the arena. They moved against the traffic flow and were making slow progress when the national anthem began. Everyone stood and faced the flag flying over the scoreboard. Some rock star Sarah could not identify belted out his own rendition of "The Star-Spangled Banner." Before he reached the last two lines, the crowd cheered, including Sarah and Marshall, Jason and Maggie.

As the roar died down, the umpire called, "Play ball," and the four reached the exit and were about to begin their descent when Marshall stopped to look back at the first batter. As he swung and missed, the home crowd cheered and the Royals were off to a good start.

"So, what's going on?" Maggie demanded again.

Sarah explained.

"Well, we can't just stand here and watch the game," Maggie said.

"Why can't we?" Sarah asked, suddenly believing that that was exactly what they could do. "People are in the aisles all the time, going to the restrooms or to the concession stands. If we get in the way, we could always walk on up the aisle, as if we're going to our seats."

Maggie leaned over and whispered in Sarah's ear. "And you said you couldn't act like a dumb blond."

Sarah ignored her. "It'll work, won't it, Marshall?" She turned beseeching eyes to him.

"I don't see why not," he assured her. "You don't get the chance to see the play-offs very often, and we're already in here."

Maggie took Jason's arm. "I could use a hot dog. Why don't we head for the concession stand?"

"It might be better if we split up," Marshall suggested. "We'd be less conspicuous that way. When the game's over, why don't we meet you at the gate where we came in?"

"Fine," Jason agreed. He and Maggie headed for the refreshment area.

Marshall put his arm around Sarah's shoulders. "Don't worry. This will be fine. I've been sitting all day. I need to stand for a while, and I'd hate to miss this game."

They leaned, side by side, against a concrete pillar beside the arena's entrance and watched the game. Marshall hailed a peddler and bought them each a hot dog and a soft drink, which they demolished quickly.

"Every half inning, let's move to another section," Marshall suggested. He placed his hands on her shoulders and steered her through the crowd to the concession area.

They decided they would stay in the general vicinity of the box, so they would have it as an excuse if they were stopped. Marshall kept a hand on Sarah, either on her shoulder, around her waist, or just held her hand. When he would pull it away to applaud or buy another cold drink, Sarah felt bereft until he touched her again. In the midst of thousands of strangers, she wanted his presence close.

As the game seesawed back and forth, the fans were on their feet most of the time, and Marshall and Sarah blended right in. During the seventh-inning stretch, they met Maggie and Jason as they strolled to another section. Jason gave the thumbs-up sign as they passed on the steps. Even Maggie seemed caught up in the fun.

At the end of the eighth inning, the game was tied at four to four. The Royals got the first three batters out in the top half of the ninth, and then took their turn at bat. The entire stadium was on its feet as the bases were loaded and two players struck out. The next batter came up and successfully bunted, and the runner on third slid on home. Safe!

The crowd roared. Marshall picked up Sarah and swung her around.

"Enough! I'm dizzy," she cried, and he set her back on her feet only to pull her close in a bear hug.

"Best game I've ever seen," he shouted over the thundering crowd.

No one was in a hurry to leave the stadium. The euphoria continued even after the field was cleared of players and excited fans. Finally, Marshall ushered Sarah toward the ticket gate where they were to meet Jason and Maggie. The other couple was waiting for them.

"Thanks for getting us in, Sarah." Jason gave her a big hug. "Terrific game."

"Yeah. It was fun," Maggie said. "Where shall we go to

celebrate? Your place, Sarah?"

"How about a small get-together at a friend's house? I know you won't know anyone, but trust me, you'll like it."

Marshall tossed her the keys. "It's your friend; you drive us there. I can't take any more of your last-second directions like on the ride out here."

"Okay. That might be easier," she said with a laugh. "Where's the car?" she asked as the foursome walked out the gate, and she was answered with three blank stares.

"If we hadn't checked so many ticket lines, I would have remembered," Jason said.

Marshall shook his head. "I haven't a clue."

They retraced their route from ticket gate to ticket gate and finally Jason spotted the right area.

It took forever to get out of the parking lot, but Sarah finally maneuvered the car through the stadium gates and onto the road. Thirty-five minutes, later she pulled to a stop at the guardhouse at Lake Quivera.

"Hi, George," she called out her open window. "Don't have the pass with me."

"No problem," the guard said and waved them through.

"What kind of place is this? Trying to keep people in or out?" Jason asked.

"It's a secure village. And could be a bit of both," Sarah said and laughed. "My parents live here as well as otherretirees who play golf every day on the courses. A lot of younger people live here, too, if they can afford it."

"And your friend can afford it?" Marshall asked.

"Yes, he can afford it."

"He?" Marshall did not like the sound of that. But she would not take him to a boyfriend's home, would she? He had not asked her if there were anyone special in her life. She had told him the doctor he had met last night meant nothing to her, but was there anyone else? He would have to straighten that out.

"He's my parents' neighbor," Sarah explained.

She followed the road that twisted around a couple of wooded hills, then crossed the bridge over Lake Quivera. After another few blocks, she turned into the wide driveway of a modern, glass-and-wood house.

"Looks like your friend's not here," Marshall said.

"This is my parents' home. My friend lives around the corner, although you can't see his house from here. All the homes must be sited so they can't be seen from other houses. The view's important." Sarah urged her companions out of the car and used her key to let them into the house.

"I thought we'd have coffee here. My friend was at the game, too, and will be just a little longer getting home."

"Your parents live here alone?" Jason asked. "Or do they keep an extra ten people around to fill the place up?"

"It's large for two, but they entertain quite a bit," Sarah said. "Maggie, show them around while I fix coffee."

"This is quite a place," Jason said a few minutes later when the men and Maggie joined Sarah in the sitting area. "Just what does your father do?"

"Dr. Stuart Madison, surgeon, now retired," Sarah answered.

"So you got your interest in medicine from him," Marshall said.

"What do you mean?" Maggie asked and cast a sharp glance at Sarah.

"Sarah's volunteer work at the hospital," Marshall answered.

"Oh, that," Maggie said, nodding in agreement.

Sarah sent a chilling look Maggie's direction. "I believe I'll phone my friend and see if he's home yet." She excused herself and returned a short time later. "He's there," she announced. "Let's go."

The foursome trouped over to Arlie's house where music poured from every window. A couple of cars were parked in the driveway.

"Looks like the party's in full swing," Jason said.

"Yes. It's a celebration because the Royals are going to the Series." Sarah marched them up to the front door, knocked once, although she was sure it would not be heard over the loud music, then opened the door without waiting for it to be answered.

She obviously knows this guy well, since she just walks right in, Marshall thought. He'd only known Sarah one day. Surely he couldn't be feeling even the tiniest bit jealous? He shrugged that thought off immediately.

"Sarah, you made it," a deep masculine voice yelled over the rock music. A man in his late twenties, with babyish good looks that were slightly familiar, hugged Sarah and spun her around. Marshall did not like it one bit. "What did you think of the game?" the man shouted.

"Wonderful, just wonderful," Sarah shouted back, laughing up at him. "Arlie, I'd like you to meet my friends. Marshall Adams, Jason Bradford, Maggie Gale, this is Arlie Gilbert."

"Arlie Gilbert? The shortstop?" Jason gasped, sticking out his hand and pumping Arlie's hand up and down.

"One and the same." Sarah watched Marshall shake hands with Arlie and laughed out loud at the look of excitement on Marshall's face.

"Come, meet my friends," Arlie said and led the small group into the large living room where three other ballplayers and their wives had gathered to celebrate the victory and rehash the details of the game.

❧

It was almost two in the morning when Sarah drove

Marshall's car back to the Missouri side of Kansas City. She dropped Maggie off at her apartment building first. Jason walked his date to her door and took a long time saying good night.

"Perhaps we'd better say good night here, too," Marshall suggested, "while we have a bit of privacy." He shoved the armrest up out of his way and pulled her over toward the passenger side and into his arms.

"I had a wonderful time, Sarah. Couldn't have been any better even if we'd had box seats," he said, grinning that boyish grin she had seen at the game and at Arlie's party.

"I'm glad you enjoyed it. I did, too."

"Good. We have that out of the way. Now let's get down to some serious good-nighting."

"Good-nighting?"

"Yes. It goes like this." His lips met hers in a kiss that made the ones the night before pale in comparison. He kissed her again as the back door of the car was being opened and, with the sound, Sarah pushed away from Marshall, ending the contact.

"Excuse me," Jason said. "Should I come back later?"

"Yes," Marshall said.

"No," Sarah said at the same time.

"Which is it?" Jason asked, still standing outside the car with the door open.

"Get in, Jason," Sarah said and laughed.

"Give her the keys to a car and the power goes to her head," Marshall teased, but he let her scoot over behind the steering wheel.

"Did you get your car fixed?" Marshall asked.

"No. Well, yes, but I was too late to get it this afternoon. I'll have to take a cab to work again tomorrow."

"You can use my car," Marshall offered. "I don't need it at the hotel. I'll catch a cab over to your house tomorrow evening, pick up my car, and take you out to dinner. There's a fleet of cabs parked outside the hotel, so it'll be much easier for me to get one than for you to get one early in the morning."

"Oh, Marshall, that's unnecessary."

"I insist. Now, chauffeur us to the hotel, please."

Sarah dropped them at the front door, and Jason quickly jumped out.

"Thanks for a wonderful time, Sarah," he echoed Marshall's earlier words.

"You're welcome," Sarah called to his retreating back.

"I think he wants us to be alone," Marshall said.

"I don't think the car waiting behind us wants that."

Marshall turned in his seat and looked back. He sighed. "Okay, but tomorrow night just you and me. Seven?"

"Perfect. I'll see you then."

He gave her a quick peck on the lips and climbed out of the car. "I had a great time," he said before he slammed the car door closed and gave it a slap, as if sending a horse on its way.

Jason, who had been standing by the door, walked back to where Marshall was watching Sarah drive off. "How much did you pay for that car?" he asked his friend.

Marshall's eyebrows rose in reaction to the odd question. "Somewhere around thirty thousand."

"You just let a woman you've known for twenty-four hours drive off in your thirty-thousand-dollar car. Are you nuts?"

Marshall's eyebrows shot up again. "I guess I am. I hadn't thought of it like that. But I trust her. I don't know why, but I do."

four

Marshall was a morning person. He had been an early riser all his life and, although he had gotten to bed late, his internal alarm buzzed him at six.

He turned over, knowing he should catch more sleep, but years of habit kept him from dozing off again. Instead, he gave up. Propping his pillows against the headboard, he leaned back and reached for the remote control that was securely fastened to the bedside table. The television sprang to life with the push of the button, and he flicked from channel to channel to find something interesting. He settled for an early morning business report on the falling value of the dollar. The newscaster droned on and did not hold his attention. When a cute, blond analyst came on the screen, she reminded him of Sarah and his thoughts never returned to the falling dollar.

Sarah was something special and he knew it. Jason may have thought it crazy that he had sent her off in the car he had had only two months, but he knew it was a simple matter of trust. There was something about her that defied easy explanations. She was classy, no question about that; she had been raised that way. The stately old house where she lived spoke volumes. And that she would not give up her childhood home, but bought it instead of looking for a modern glass-and-chrome place, told him about her sense of loyalty. He had not been in her home long the night before. Tonight he would get a tour and notice all the little touches that made it fit her personality.

The sound of downtown traffic reached his ears even though it was still early. City life. What a difference. His thoughts drifted to the Valley, his home in the country.

In the twenties, the story went, gangsters and underworld figures from Chicago wanted vacation getaway places in the Ozark Hills. The Valley was started as such a place. The steep hills had been terraced and, from a distance, resembled stair steps for giants. A huge resort was planned, but only the first home was built before something happened to halt the project. Some said a gangster was gunned down and his widow would never return to the hills where he had been killed. Others said the developer went bankrupt. Marshall preferred the first story.

The original place had fallen into disrepair. All the glass had been broken out by vandals long before Marshall had been born. The first time he had seen it, the roof had already caved in. But he had fallen in love with the feeling of the Valley and when, years later, he had returned to Neosho as a doctor, he immediately inquired about the place.

Buying it was a lengthy process; the title was still held by someone in Chicago. But eventually it was his. The rotten timbers of the old place were bulldozed out and his A-frame home was built on its old foundation, nestled in a valley and surrounded by the terraced hills.

What would Sarah think of his home? She would like it; he knew she would. She might be a city girl, but she would fall in love with the country and be happy there.

What was he thinking? Sure, she might seem like the woman of his dreams, but he had known her only a short time. He did not even know where she taught or much else about her. She had certainly been embarrassed last night when the box seats had been taken, but she would not confront her dad's friends. She had carefully avoided being seen by them. He liked that. She would not put them in an awkward position because she had misunderstood about the tickets.

He might not know much about Sarah's everyday existence, but he knew her inner qualities. And he liked them. Couple them with her stunning appearance, and it seemed an unbelievable combination.

She had called Arlie and arranged the meeting with the ballplayer so that Marshall could have a special night. Arlie had pulled him aside at the party and had given him a friendly warning about her.

"Treat her right or answer to me," he had said in a joking way, but Marshall knew he meant it.

He would treat her right, and he wanted to talk to her. Glancing at his watch on the bedside table, he saw it was not quite seven. Too early to call. But then, she had said she had an early morning. If she were not up already, she should be, he decided.

There was no listing for Sarah Madison in the phone book, but there was one for Dr. S. B. Madison at Sarah's address. Obviously she had not been in the house long since the phone was still listed in her father's name. He hoped it was the right number. With a quick shrug, he poked the numbers and waited nervously as it rang once, twice, three times.

"Hello," she answered.

"Good morning, Sarah." It was wonderful to hear her voice. It sounded huskier than usual.

"Marshall?"

"Yes. Did I wake you?"

"No. I was about to have breakfast."

"I was wondering if there was any place special you would like to go tonight and if I needed to call for reservations."

"Let me think. Wednesday. It seems there was something. . .Oh, I know. Tonight is the opening of a new exhibit at the Nelson Art Gallery. Since it's a 'must' for tourists, and I had planned on going before I had the good fortune to meet you, why don't we take it in? Then go to the Savoy for a late dinner."

"Sounds wonderful. Reservations?"

"Be best. Probably around nine."

"I'll take care of it. And I'll see you at seven."

"That would be perfect. Oh, Marshall. The event is formal. Black tie. Is that a problem?"

Of course it was a problem. He had not packed formal gear to bring to a convention of doctors. The banquet Saturday night required a suit, but not a tux.

"Oh, that'll be fine. I'll see you tonight, Sarah."

She said good-bye, and he sat on the bed, holding the phone for a moment.

"No problem. Hah!" he said aloud. He flipped through the yellow pages until he found the rental places. He had no idea which one to call, and besides it was way too early. Best to shower and shave, then get advice from the hotel desk. They could tell him a good florist, too, so he could send roses to Sarah. Oh, no! He had forgotten to ask her where she taught. Well, tonight he would find out all about her.

❧

Sarah hung up the phone and smiled to herself. Marshall was a dear, sweet man like her father, and not at all like most doctors she had met. Why was it some doctors felt as if they were godlike? They had studied plenty, that was true, but it wasn't as if they could cure people by themselves. They relied on treatments, medicines, operations, things that other people had developed. And ultimately the outcome was in God's hands. Doctors were merely practitioners, like lawyers or architects, practicing what had been taught to them.

Hal Mosley was a perfect example of the typical doctor. If a patient got well, he took all the credit. If the patient died, there was nothing he could have done for him, he was too far gone before Hal saw him. It was not his fault.

Marshall did not seem that way. He seemed to be the type who tried hard, no matter what the odds, and who would mourn with the family of the victim. Marshall had talked little of his profession, but she had picked up bits and pieces. She had overheard him tell Jason that he called in every day to make sure his patients were doing all right. When she could finally tell him about her job, they could exchange their philosophies of healing, and she was sure they would be the same.

On reflection, it might be a good thing she could not tell him she was a doctor. She was getting to know him for herself, as a woman, and not as a professional. Yet she felt instinctively that he would respect her as a professional, too.

Jeff had not. They had met her senior year in college, then she had gone on to medical school. He resented the hours she spent studying and at the hospital; he never saw her enough, he had said. She should not have been surprised when he started seeing other women. Although she had thought she loved him, she would have survived it better if he had been honest and had said he thought they were too different to ever make a lasting commitment.

Instead, he had played her along as a sucker. One evening after a long day at the hospital, Sarah had dropped by his apartment, something she had not done before. One of the patients had died and she needed to see him, needed to be held, needed to know that life went on. Another woman had answered the door. She was petite and brunette, her opposite, but Sarah had not stuck around long enough to find out if the woman threatened Jeff on an intellectual level.

She found that out later when Jeff came pounding on her door. She had stepped outside and talked to him, or rather listened, as he ranted about how cold she was, how she thought she was so much smarter than he was, and how she would never be the woman Melinda was.

Stunned through and through, Sarah had somehow managed to maintain a stoic composure as he told her what he thought of her.

"Good-bye, Jeff," she had finally said when he had exhausted his supply of words. Then she had stepped back into her apartment and locked the door.

She had never seen him again and thought she had learned the lesson he had taught her. But later she had dated Troy, and he had been turned out of the same mold. Men liked intelligent women as friends, but not as marriage material. Males had to be macho to prove their masculinity, and they did not like intelligent women in a relationship.

But she might have been too hasty in drawing that conclusion. Marshall did not seem to fit that pattern at all.

He had a rugged look, high cheekbones, and a strong nose. Years of that wonderful grin had formed crinkle lines around his eyes. But it was more than that. It was the look in his eyes that said he was not surprised by much and that he was prepared for anything.

But his personality was not rugged in the typical sense of the word. He was polished and sensitive. And she would get to see him tonight. Too bad he was leaving in a few more days.

Oh, what was she thinking? Her life ran smoothly as it was and she was happy. She did not need a man complicating it. Long ago she had concluded that she was meant to remain single. She had seen how hard it was for doctors to combine family life and all those hours at the hospital. Her father had juggled as best he could, but there were times when he did not make it home. Her tenth birthday party came to mind and she quickly dismissed it. She understood now.

She sat at the kitchen table and thanked God for a new morning and a new beginning, then she quickly ate a piece of toast. Her thoughts had slowed down her normal brisk morning routine, and she was running late. Annoyed with herself for dallying, she rushed out the kitchen door that led to the garage and stopped short, staring at Marshall's car. She had forgotten that she had not picked up her car yet.

"I don't have to pretend to be a dumb blond," she said aloud. "I am one."

Sarah climbed behind the wheel of Marshall's car and drove to work. As soon as she entered the hospital, she began her rounds. Although the nurses took vitals and kept the charts current, she checked each patient three times a day. Even with a disease like leukemia, the look in the eyes and the color of the skin were indicators that were not easily communicated on a chart.

First stop was to see Andrea, who was still sleeping. Her mother sat beside her bed, holding the little girl's hand.

"Doctor?" Mrs. Garren's eyes pleaded for a word of assurance, but Sarah could give none.

"Stay with her," Sarah said. "I'll have the cafeteria send meals up for you. Your husband?"

"He went home for the night. He is going to work until noon unless I call him."

Sarah walked to the doorway and motioned for Mrs. Garren to join her.

"Call him," Sarah said in a low voice. "It may not be today, but her system can't fight it much longer."

Mrs. Garren nodded and, zombielike, walked to the bedside table. She reached for the phone, but fumbled the receiver, and it hit the floor with a loud clank. Andrea opened her eyes, bright with fever.

"Good morning, you little scamp," Sarah said tenderly. "Did you have a good night?"

Andrea smiled. "I dreamed about my new doll." She turned her head slowly on the pillow, as if her strength had been zapped. On one side of her was the new doll and on the other was the doll she had had for years. "I should put Sarah next to Tammy. They're sisters now," she explained.

Sarah placed the new doll next to Tammy. "I believe they like each other."

Andrea smiled again, but did not speak.

"Mrs. Garren, I'll make that call for you, if you'd like," Sarah volunteered. She did not want to talk to Andrea's father, but Mrs. Garren did not look as if she could handle it at the moment and certainly not in front of Andrea.

"Yes, please, Doctor."

"I'll be back later. Rest, honey," Sarah said and patted Andrea's foot.

At the nurses' station, Sarah had meals ordered for Mr. and Mrs. Garren and caught Mr. Garren just as he was about to leave his house. She explained the grave situation, then quickly made the rest of her rounds.

When she got to the lab, Dr. Lewis was already there, peeking through a microscope. He was a small man of around sixty, with gray hair and wire-rimmed glasses.

"We're losing Andrea Garren," he said without preamble.

"Yes, Doctor. I've called her family in."

He nodded. "You're good at that." At her look of disbelief he continued, "I know you hate it. Nobody likes telling parents their child is dying. But you're good at it. You let them know it hurts you, too."

"It does hurt me," Sarah whispered.

"I know. Fluconazole and itraconazole aren't fighting her infection." He deftly focused on their research. "Why does it help some and not others?"

"That's why we're here," Sarah answered. "We'll find out." She shrugged out of her white rounds jacket and into her lab coat and began examining blood samples collected earlier that morning.

An hour and a half later, Sarah reached for the ringing phone; she had a visitor in the lab station. Sarah pulled off her tight, disposable gloves and walked out to the lab desk. She recognized Maggie's red hair before her friend turned to face her.

"Hi, Maggie. I'd forgotten you were coming by this morning. Have you met with the auxiliary about the fashion show?"

"Yes. Those old gals drive me crazy."

"Keep it down, will you?" Sarah said. "Those women keep this hospital running. Research takes a great deal of money, and they raise a bundle."

Maggie looked around for any conspicuous pink jackets then whispered, "I still don't like working with them. Got time for a cup of coffee?" she asked in a more normal voice.

"A few minutes." Sarah led the way to the doctors' lounge and poured each of them a cup. They took a table by the window overlooking a water fountain, surrounded by bright flowers.

"So, what are you and Marshall doing tonight?" Maggie asked.

"We're going to the opening of the traveling Renoir exhibit at the Nelson. Then a late dinner at the Savoy."

"Wow. Fancy. If we tag along, Jason will naturally ask . . . to go with Marshall to the fashion show, if we set it up that we're a foursome. We'll come with you."

"No, you won't. I want to get to know Marshall without a crowd around."

"A double date is hardly a crowd."

"Too crowded for me."

"And what exactly is it you want to know about him you can't find out with an audience, Sarah?" Maggie asked.

"I just like talking to him alone. Why don't you go over to Ellen's and play games or something like that? But then, they'll probably be at the exhibit. There are a thousand other things around the city for you to do."

"Yes, but the art gallery on opening night sounds so sophisticated. I'll bet they'll have caviar."

"Probably. But it's black tie and by invitation, and you're not going to use me to succeed on your dare." Suddenly her heart sank. She would know several of the people there. She should never have invited Marshall. Now she would have to dodge people. Oh, she'd better call her brother. He would be there and could blow her bet if she did not warn him.

"Black tie," Maggie said thoughtfully. "Last night was fun. Even standing up, the game was exciting. How'd you get Arlie to invite us to his party?"

"Arlie wanted to meet Marshall. The victory made it a great party."

"I guess! It would have been a wake if the Royals had lost that game." Maggie downed the last of her coffee. "Well, I won't keep you. I know you're busy, and I've got to get downtown to deliver designs for next week's windows. We have a new window dresser who breaks an arm off mannequins by just looking at them." She stood up and tucked her envelope handbag under her arm. "Have you asked Marshall to the fashion show yet?"

"No," Sarah said as she walked Maggie toward the front entrance. "I was hoping to ask him tonight."

"I might mention the show. Lay the groundwork so he'll want to go. I like him, Sarah." Maggie did not explain who "him" was, but her soft tone said it for her.

"I know. Jason's a nice man. I like his friend," she admitted.

"We've found a couple of fine fellows, Sarah. Jason's had two failed marriages, and he's a little cynical, but the more I learn about him, the more I like him."

"Marshall thinks a lot of him," Sarah said. "And I trust his judgment. See you." Sarah waved as Maggie opened the outside door, then she walked purposefully to Andrea's room.

Mr. Garren sat beside his wife, his hands gripping the arms of the chair, his knuckles white. Andrea was asleep again. Sarah asked them to step into the hall.

"Has she talked in the last hour?"

Mrs. Garren looked up. "Yes. She's just now dozed off again."

"When she wakes, call a nurse. I'd like another blood sample," Sarah said briskly.

"Why, doctor? If there's no hope?"

"What we learn from Andrea might save another little girl," Sarah said as matter-of-factly as she could, although she hated causing Andrea any more pain. She did not know how to act with families during the waiting period before death. Dr. Lewis might think she was good at it, but she knew she was awful.

"I'll be back later. Remember, call the nurse when she awakens again."

Sarah gave instructions at the nurses' station and returned to the lab. She met Hal coming out of his office.

"Glad I caught you, Sarah. Have you forgotten we were going over to the convention for the session on pediatrics?"

"It slipped my mind. Let me check out with Dr. Lewis." The renowned physician had asked her to call him Warner, but she could not bring herself to do it. Somehow it sounded disrespectful. She spoke with him briefly, then met Hal in the hall.

"Let's take my car," Sarah suggested. "Actually it's a friend's car. We can pick up my car at the garage on the way, and I'll leave his at the hotel."

"Let me guess. Dr. Marshall Adams?" Hal said as they walked to the parking lot.

"You have a good memory. Would you mind driving my car to the hotel for me?"

"Sure. Your friend was kind enough to let you borrow his until yours was fixed, right?"

"Something like that." She slipped behind the wheel and Hal climbed in on the passenger's side. He made no secret of the fact that he did not like being driven around by a woman.

"Relax, Hal. We're almost there." Almost to where Marshall was. Panic hit her briefly and she calmed herself. There were thousands at the convention and sessions going on in other meeting areas as well as at the main hotel. Marshall would not attend a workshop on pediatrics, or would he? He was a general practitioner, a much-needed family doctor, and a conscientious one. Wouldn't he want to learn what he could do for all of his patients, no matter what their age?

Hal had opened his leather-bound legal pad and flipped through some papers that were stuck under the flap on the left side.

"The session starts in ten minutes," he said, waving a schedule of meetings at her. "In the Maple Room."

"We'll make it." Sarah whipped the car into the garage parking lot. "Come with me, and we'll be out of here faster."

Inside the garage, Sarah scribbled a check to the mechanic and handed Hal the keys. The mechanic wanted to talk to her about the car, so Sarah motioned for Hal to go on and drive her car to the hotel.

"I'll meet you there," she called after him.

The mechanic explained what he had done to the car and kept Sarah a couple of minutes. When she pulled Marshall's car into the stream of traffic, her little Miata was nowhere in sight.

At the hotel, Sarah parked in the underground parking lot and took the elevator to the lobby. As she got off, the first person she saw was Marshall. He was talking to three men and a woman as the group walked away from the bank of elevators toward the meeting rooms. Sarah could see only the woman from the back, but quickly noticed how she walked closer to Marshall than was necessary down the wide halls. She wore a feminine, pink dress, had her long dark hair pulled back and tied with a pink scarf, and had on unnecessarily high heels for a casual session at the conference. Sarah's first reaction was to claw the other woman's eyes out. She was shocked that she could have such a violent response to the striking female. She was even more stunned that she thought of the woman in certain terms, and none of them were respectful.

Marshall and his little group stood outside the Cedar Room, continuing their discussion. Instead of walking past him to her meeting room, Sarah ducked into the first door she passed. Unfortunately, it was a janitor's closet.

A single, white bulb hung from a cord in the center of the closet. A deep, white porcelain sink, bare pipes exposed below it, hung low from the wall. An assortment of mops and brooms hung from the opposite wall.

After a minute, Sarah peeked out. Marshall was still there. The men had disappeared, but the woman in pink remained, hanging onto every word Marshall uttered. He looked around as if he felt her eyes on him, and Sarah ducked back into the closet.

She waited another long moment. Then, as she was turning the handle to open the door, it was jerked open from the outside. Her heart jumped to her throat.

A young man in a janitor's uniform sprang back in alarm. Sarah put her finger to her lips is a request for silence. As soon as the man had his wits about him, his whole demeanor changed. A sly smirk told her he had misread the situation. Surely the man would not take her hiding in the closet as a come-on? And yet it seemed that that was exactly what he thought. He stepped into the tiny room and closed the door behind him. Sarah stepped back until she was against the wall. He moved closer, inching toward her in slow motion. Sarah suddenly gave him a hard push in the chest, which caught him off guard, and he sank down into the deep sink as easily as if he had sat in a chair, his legs dangling over the edge.

Rushing out the door, Sarah dashed down the now empty hall. The sessions had started. She found the Maple Room, opened the door, and slipped in. Hal was sitting in the back row with an empty seat beside him. Thankfully, she slid into the chair.

She did not hear a word of the talk by the famous television pediatrician. Was that episode in the closet really her fault? Had her signal for silence been misinterpreted? No, surely she was in the clear. That man had been a slimy worm. Maybe she should not have been in the closet, but he could have asked her why she was there instead of assuming the worst. He was lower than a slimy worm. Yet, he had not done anything to her. Maybe her imagination was working overtime.

By the time the question and answer period was halfway over, Sarah had calmed down. She borrowed a sheet of paper from Hal and wrote Marshall a note.

As the final applause died, Sarah jumped from her chair and started for the door with Hal in tow. Like a spy from a B-grade movie, she stuck her head into the hall and looked both ways before stepping out of the room. This time she was avoiding two men, or rather, one man and one worm. Hal, looking bewildered, followed her antics but Sarah ignored him. With a brisk pace, she marched to the check-in desk, asked for an envelope, wrote his name on it in her clear script, and tucked her note and Marshall's keys in it. She shoved the envelope back across the desk and asked that Marshall be notified that he had a message.

Sarah twirled away from the desk and immediately spotted the young janitor lounging at the entrance to a corridor a few feet away. She froze for a second, but his expletive, "Crazy woman!" said in a voice loud enough to carry to those around them, made her spring into action. She grabbed Hal by the arm and stalked to the stairs that led to the parking garage.

"Where are we parked?" she demanded.

"This way," he said. "What's wrong with you, Sarah?"

"Nothing," she snapped. "I have lots to do today. Covering for the other doctors so that they can lollygag at this convention is wearing me thin."

"Sarah, you agreed to cover so others could attend more sessions. And there are some top-notch physicians here. Didn't you listen to one word Dr. Alexander said today?"

"Of course, I did."

"Then you understand the importance of sharing information with each other. Sarah, you're in research.

You know that."

"Yes, I do." She held out her hand. "Keys?"

"Your car handles well. I'll drive," he said.

"I'll drive my own car, thank you." She was startled by the force behind her words. Hal was her friend who had helped her out countless times. He was handsome and intelligent, and he had better shut up and give her the keys before she did something she could not predict.

Hal unlocked his door, handed her the keys, and climbed into the passenger's seat, slamming the door behind him. Sarah did the same on the driver's side.

What was wrong with her? She felt like calling Hal every name in the book. *Sanctimonious jerk* topped the list, and she wasn't even sure if *sanctimonious* fit. It sounded good in her mind, but she was too smart to say it out loud.

They rode to the hospital in a heavy silence, finally broken by Sarah.

"I'm sorry. I've got a lot on my mind. I didn't mean to take it out on you."

"What's wrong, Sarah?" Hal reached over and patted her hand, which lay on the seat.

She jerked her hand away to downshift and she turned the sports car into the hospital parking lot.

"I have a patient who's not going to make it."

"Sarah," he said as if talking to a child who had not learned her lesson in school. "Patients die here every day. We get the worst cases in this part of the state. You've got to learn to deal with that."

She nodded and bit her tongue to keep from yelling, "You sanctimonious jerk!" at the top of her lungs.

five

Marshall smiled and nodded absently. Dr. Kerry Webster from Boston had leeched onto him early that morning in the hotel dining room before he had had his first cup of coffee. It was almost noon, and she was still beside him.

How could he get rid of her? The subtle approach had not worked; a ton of bricks probably would not do it, either.

They were strolling toward the lobby after a particularly long session. Marshall needed to slip out and run his errand to the tuxedo rental shop, but he did not want to be rude.

"Shall we have lunch downtown instead of here at the hotel?" Kerry asked in her honeyed voice.

Marshall looked closely at her. Kerry was soft looking. Her pink dress gave her a very feminine look, but her gray eyes revealed a streak of steel behind the womanly appearance. Rude was the only thing that would work with her.

"Sorry, I've already made plans. If you'll excuse me." Marshall spun around and walked the opposite direction. He had intended to inquire at the desk about a nearby shop, but he would ask the cab driver instead. He slipped out a side door and hailed a cab.

While the driver maneuvered through lunchtime traffic toward the nearest rental shop, Marshall sat back and thought about doctors in general and women doctors in particular. If Kerry was a typical woman doctor and, from his limited contact with female doctors he tended to think she was, he did not like them. Many men were in the profession for the money or the prestige. Women were in it for both those reasons and to prove they could tackle what was once an all-male profession. He knew there were some men, and begrudgingly he admitted some women, who were dedicated to healing, unconcerned with the perks of the job. He liked to believe he was one of them.

The cab pulled up to the curb, and the driver charged an exorbitant amount, but it had been a long ride.

The shop was not crowded, and Marshall was measured and fitted in a matter of minutes. Holding the hanger with two fingers, he slung the tuxedo bag over his back and began walking north, all the while watching for a cab.

There were not many events in Marshall's life that had called for a tuxedo. Mainly weddings. He smiled as he remembered one in Chicago when he was a groomsman. The church was not far from the hospital, and he had driven his motorcycle over and changed there, not thinking about the reception, which was scheduled for a posh country club. He was going on duty at the hospital and could not stay long at the reception, so he did not think he should inconvenience anyone by hitching a ride in a car. Instead, he had bundled up his regular clothes and tied them on his bike. He had thought he would be embarrassed, riding a motorcycle in a tux, but he had felt the most exhilarating high, as if he were defying convention, flaunting society. It was a feeling he liked, and he was not a rebel at heart. The motorcycle was not a statement against society; it was an economic move. His old clunker car had guzzled gas the way a teenager drank Coke. One dream, for when he got his own practice, was for a new car. He did not need a Mercedes or a Porsche, his Lincoln fit the bill. It was all the luxury he needed, and it was his third brand-new car.

He waited for the crossing light to tell him to walk, wishing he had his car right now. Maybe he had been foolish letting Sarah drive it to her house the night before, instead of putting her in a cab.

A cab. He waved with his free hand, and the approaching cabbie pulled up. Marshall climbed into the backseat and gave the name of his hotel.

The cabbie looked him over and said, "You're the boss. That tux heavy?"

"Not particularly," Marshall answered. Had he gotten one of those cabbies who would talk about anything? He settled back in his seat as the cab driver turned left and then left again at the next block.

"Here you are," the driver said.

Marshall was silent for a moment while he tried to get his temper under control. "You might say I've been taken for a ride. I asked another driver to take me to the closest rental shop, and he drove me around for twenty minutes."

"You just can't trust everybody these days," the cabbie offered his advice.

Marshall agreed and tried to think of something other than how he had been cheated. He did not like being taken for a fool. It was the worst feeling in the world. He had trusted someone who was untrustworthy, and he was usually a better judge of character than that. He should have watched the way the driver had gone, and maybe he would have noticed when he had doubled back.

Marshall paid the driver and carried the tux through the lobby to the stairs. He had found the stairs a good way to get some exercise while he was at the convention and a way to avoid offensive doctors. There were probably no more obnoxious people in his profession than in any other but, in his present mood, it seemed that way to him.

The moment he entered his room, he saw the flashing

light on his phone. He called the front desk and was informed he had a note in his box. Once more he entered the stairwell, this time descending to the lobby. The clerk handed over the envelope, telling him a woman had left if over an hour ago.

Marshall climbed the stairs again and in the quiet of his room sat down and opened the envelope. His car keys fell out. He read the brief note from Sarah, then checked his watch. His car had been parked at the hotel the entire time he had been searching for a cab.

From there on, his day went downhill. His daily call to his office told him that one of his older patients, who should have been released from the hospital, had relapsed and had developed pneumonia. Although the doctor taking over his patients for the week was very competent, had it not been for Sarah, he would have packed his bags and left for home.

He did not feel he was getting out of this convention what he had anticipated. It was his first national convention and since it was so close to home, he thought he should attend it. Some new procedures and drugs were presented, and that was beneficial, but the event was more political than geared toward learning, and his attitude toward the people around him detracted from the informal sessions.

He did not know why he had such a bad attitude toward these other doctors. It was great seeing Jason again. Ed, he could take in small doses, and he had had enough already. Women like Kerry rubbed him the wrong way, too.

His growling stomach told him it was past time for lunch, so he walked to the mom-and-pop deli he had seen next to the hotel. He ordered pastrami on rye and iced tea and sat at a window table watching the traffic, both in cars and on foot. There was something lonely about seeing so many people and not knowing a single one. No one to say "hi" and call out his name.

The afternoon session was an election of national officers. It went on and on, like a political convention, with nominating speeches and acceptance speeches. Marshall was not a political animal; he did not seek the spotlight or awards that seemed shallow or insignificant. He felt like an outsider, but he was called upon to pass out and collect ballots, so he could not leave.

Later, dressed in the tux, he admired himself in the mirror. He was not vain, but he knew he was good-looking. Enough women had told him so. And tonight he was glad for he wanted to look good for Sarah. His spirits were beginning to climb as he drove his car out of the parking garage toward Sarah's home. He flipped up the armrest that divided the two front seats and discovered Sarah's checkbook caught underneath it. Her purse must have spilled while she was driving.

He pulled into her driveway, parked, and picked up the checkbook to return to its owner. Out of curiosity, he opened it to see which checks she had picked. Somehow he figured her for the standard, wavy blue-lined type, no fuss, no frills. Just class.

Instead, a family crest and the name of Dr. Harold C. Mosley jumped out at him. Sarah's friend he had met at the coffeehouse Monday night. What was Mosley's checkbook doing in his car?

Marshall poked the doorbell twice.

As soon as she heard the bell, Sarah opened the door with a welcoming smile. Marshall stood there resplendent in formal wear with a thunderous look on his face and a deep frown line between his blue eyes.

"I believe your friend left this in my car," he said without a word of greeting. He stalked into the large entry hall before Sarah could ask him in.

Sarah took the checkbook from his outstretched hand and opened it. A quick replay in her mind of the morning ride assured her Hal had dropped it when he was shuffling through papers searching for the location of the session.

"This morning Hal wanted to attend a session at the convention, so I persuaded him to go with me to the garage and drive my car to the hotel, while I followed in yours. I parked your car, got mine, and drove back to work. I'm sorry. I should have asked permission before driving your car so much."

"That's all right," Marshall said, waving his hand as if dismissing her apology. "But why Mosley? I thought he didn't mean anything to you." He was probably blowing it; he did not mean to sound jealous, but he was, and he knew it was showing.

"Hal was going to the hotel, and I was going to drop your car off there," Sarah explained. She hoped he would not ask how Hal planned to get back to the hospital.

"What were you doing at the hospital?" He seemed to be mollified by her answers, but he kept prying.

"Andrea Garren is a special little girl, and she's dying. I've become attached to her, and I wanted to see her."

How insensitive can I be? Marshall thought. He knew he could trust her, knew it instinctively, yet here he was giving her the third degree about nothing important when she was facing the death of a friend. That episode with the cab driver had him distrusting even her.

"Sarah, I'm sorry I've been such a bear. I've not had a good day, and I can tell that you haven't, either."

"What's gone wrong with your day?"

"Several things." He counted on his fingers. "I got cornered by a woman doctor and couldn't get rid of her. A cab driver took me ten miles out of my way so he could raise the fare. The session this afternoon was an absolute waste of time. I have an elderly patient at home who's developed pneumonia. That's enough. I won't bore you with the rest."

"You don't like women doctors?" Sarah asked. She was glad he had not wanted to be with the woman in pink, and she felt sure that that was the woman doctor he was talking about."I guess you could say that," he said glumly. "Most of them are in medicine just to prove that they're just as smart as men."

"And aren't they?" Sarah's voice was rising. Her day had not been all candy and roses and she did not need the same song, different verse, from Marshall as she had had from Hal. And both were variations of Jeff's favorite theme.

"Well, I can see I'm not doing well here. Let's just say that at this conference I've had my fill of doctors, men and women. I'm not a chauvinist, Sarah, although I realize I sound like one. Let's forget this conversation and begin again. Okay?" He pivoted and walked back to the front door, opened it, and went outside, leaving an open-mouthed Sara, standing at the foot of the oak staircase, staring at the door.

The doorbell rang, and Sarah smiled at his ploy. Again she walked to the door and opened it. Marshall stood outside with a wide grin.

"Good evening, Sarah. You look ravishing." And she did. How could he have ignored that fact before? Her navy blue beaded gown clung in all the right places and made the blond in front of him look magnificent.

"Thank you. You look very handsome. Please, come in." She was glad they had started over. She had spent more time than normal dressing up in her finery and had pulled her blond hair back on one side, securing it with a jeweled comb, to give her a more sophisticated look. She liked the way she looked and she liked the effect her appearance had on Marshall. She could see it in his eyes, the male appreciation, and not for a moment did she view it as a chauvinistic look. He looked at her as a man looked at a woman he admired and desired, and she knew she was looking at him in the same way. Marshall closed the door and immediately took Sarah in his arms. He held her close for a long moment, then he kissed her. One kiss melted into another.

Sarah was the one to break contact. "I think we'd better be going," she said.

Marshall continued holding her, although he did not kiss her again. He pressed her head to his shoulder and held her. Finally, he let her go.

"I'll get my purse," Sarah said and escaped up the stairs to her bedroom to repair her lipstick.

Left alone downstairs, Marshall wandered through French doors into the living room. The room was comfortable, dominated by a large, stone fireplace at one end. Bookcases on one wall held an assortment of books, mostly mysteries and lots of bric-a-brac. It was not the dime store variety of what-nots; it was classic stuff. An antique camera held the place of honor on one shelf, a bouquet of dried wheat on another. He stopped in front of a huge glass jar with a glass lid, which was full of hard butterscotch candies.

"Help yourself," Sarah said, as she entered the room.

"Don't mind if I do." Marshall lifted the lid carefully and picked out two of the cellophane-wrapped candies. He offered one to Sarah who immediately accepted it. "So, you have a sweet tooth," Marshall observed.

"No, not one. A whole mouthful." Sarah chuckled. "Don't warn me, doctor. I know the danger. I keep it around all the time and because it's here, I don't seem to crave it like I did when it wasn't available. Sounds crazy, doesn't it?"

"Not if it works." He pointed to a bust of a young girl, which was painted a fiery red. "Is it you?" There was a vague resemblance.

"It's me at twelve. My oldest brother made it in high school art class."

"I didn't know you had a brother."

"Two brothers, Matt and Joe, both older than me, and my younger sister, Annie. Matt will be at the exhibit tonight. Joe lives in Washington, D.C., and works for the diplomatic service."

"Impressive. Has he been out of the country much?"

"Many times. He speaks fluent Spanish so is in demand in the South American countries. Right now he's on R and R back in the States, but he's going to Argentina in February."

Sarah reached down and turned on a lamp. A soft puddle of light fell at her feet. "We'll leave this one on," she explained as she flicked a switch that turned off the wall lights. "Ready?"

"Yes. Lead me to another of Kansas City's wonders. But I don't believe it can top last night's," he warned as he followed her out to his car.

Sarah smiled to herself as she let Marshall hand her into the passenger's seat. She was glad he had enjoyed the ball game, but felt confident he would also like the Nelson Art Gallery. It was one of her favorite places, especially on a rainy Sunday afternoon. Tonight the mood would be different; a gala party atmosphere would fill the place. Sarah liked the special openings, too. Dressing up made her feel elegant and having a special man at her side was something she had looked forward to all day.

She gave Marshall directions, and soon they were entering the mammoth doors of the museum. Sarah handed her invitation to the doorman.

"This is an impressive building," Marshall observed as they wandered among a couple hundred other guests in the gigantic open lobby. Marble columns, three feet in diameter, reached to the ceiling three or four stories above them.

"As they say, you ain't seen nothin' yet," Sarah said with a laugh. "There are four wings to this building, which join to form a square. Inside the square is a garden, where they'll have refreshments. The exhibit of Renoir's work will be in the west part of this wing where traveling exhibits are displayed. Follow me."

"I'd follow you anywhere," Marshall said and winked at her.

Sarah took his arm. As they walked into the Renoir room, she was aware that many women turned for a second look at her escort, and her heart soared that she was the one with him.

It was not just his good looks that attracted her, although they certainly did not detract. It was his inner qualities. Oh, he had shown flashes of male chauvinism, but it would be hard to find a man who did not have a few of the characteristics that society had force-fed him. He was not like Jeff. Or was she wanting to believe that because she was falling under his spell?

They slowly toured the collection, pausing longer in front of a few paintings and passing quickly over others. Their tastes were similar and Sarah enjoyed discussing the paintings with Marshall.

"I don't know a lot about art," Marshall confessed. "Shall I say the cliché, which happens to be true? I just know what I like."

"I'm the same way," Sarah confessed. "I'd like to think

I was a connoisseur of fine art, but that's not true. Some pictures make me feel a certain way and even if it isn't a feeling I like, if I feel an emotion, then I think it's good art."

"Sarah," a husky, masculine voice called, and Marshall cringed to think there was another male friend of Sarah's he would have to meet.

A portly gentleman, red-complexioned and with a thin mustache that looked incongruous on his large face, greeted Sarah with a hug. Marshall gave a deep sigh of relief, which was short-lived.

"Dewey, I'd like you to meet Marshall Adams. Marshall, Dewey Applebey. Dewey's a great patron of the arts and a longtime family friend." She doubted Dewey would give her job away. He liked talking about himself too much.

"For a moment there I thought you were going to say 'old' family friend," Dewey said as he shook hands with Marshall.

"Never," Sarah replied. "Should you live to be two hundred, you'd still not be old."

"I knew I liked this gal," Dewey said, placing his arm around Sarah's shoulders. "What sort of work do you do, Marshall?"

From the look in the man's eyes, Marshall decided Dewey was a lecherous old man—who had better get his hands off Sarah.

"I'm a doctor," Marshall answered.

"Ah. Keeping it in the family, huh, Sarah?" He squeezed her shoulder with his fat hand, and Marshall had to bite his tongue to keep from telling the man to leave her alone.

"Dad would like that," Sarah said, to cover Dewey's remark. She could tell that Marshall did not like Dewey, even though he was smiling and saying all the polite things. She excused them, saying they were headed to the garden.

The two men shook hands again, and Marshall escorted Sarah to the inner courtyard where a string quartet played.

"So, why don't you like Dewey?" Sarah asked after they had filled plates from the hors d'oeuvre table and found a bench in a corner.

"He's a dirty old man," Marshall said shortly.

"You're right. I don't know why my parents put up with him. He's been married four times, and each bride gets younger."

"Stay away from him," Marshall ordered, then realized by the little flare in her eyes and the lift of her chin that his tone of voice had not set well with her.

"I didn't mean that like it sounded. I just don't like that man, and I hope you don't have to be around him very much." Marshall hoped that would appease her. He had already been chauvinistic tonight, and his jealous words were giving away too much of his feelings toward her. And he did not even know what his feelings were.

He watched Sarah, who nodded acceptance of his words. "I'm very sensitive today. The least little thing tends to set me off. Sorry. I'll try to be more easygoing."

Sarah's eyes suddenly got large.

"What?" he asked immediately.

"Duck back here," she directed and stepped behind an oriental shrub.

"What is it?"

"It's who, not what. Maggie and Jason are here," she hissed. How had Maggie gotten in?

"So, why are we hiding?"

"Because," she started, then stopped. "Because I was hoping we could get to know each other better without them along," she blurted out. She could not tell him the truth, that she did not want Maggie using them as a constant foursome so Maggie could succeed at her dare. And yet, she had told a different truth by telling him she wanted to be alone with him. Things were getting very confusing, and she was not finding out much about him. He was sounding so typically male tonight, instead of understanding. All in all, it had been an upsetting day.

Marshall was smiling. "I want to know you better, too, Sarah. And you're right. They have been with us too much. If we're careful, we can avoid them. Where are they now?"

Sarah peeked through the leaves of the bush and spied Maggie's black dress and flaming hair by the hors d'oeuvre table

"Oh, no, they're heading this way."

"Come with me," Marshall instructed and led her to a bench on the back side of another group of shrubs. "We'll be safe here. Too bad there aren't some big trees around."

"I know. Oriental shrubs are pretty, but not the hide-behind variety. Can you see them?"

"No, and I'm not going to look. If we stare at them, they'll sense it and notice us. So, let's sit here and get to know each other better. Although I'd hoped to get to know you in private, without several hundred people milling around," he teased.

His grin was infectious, and Sarah found herself grinning back. They were two against the world, well, at least two against two others, and it felt great to be lighthearted and adventurous instead of serious and responsible.

"What would you like to know about me?" Sarah asked.

"Some things I can't find out right now," he answered with a playful leer. "Like are you ticklish behind the ear? But I'll settle for where you teach."

six

"Oh," Sarah said, unprepared for that question. Where did she teach?

"Shh," Marshall warned, before she could think up something that was not a lie. "Listen," he whispered in her ear.

"There's quite a crowd here." Jason's voice carried to where they sat hidden from view. He was standing a couple of feet in front of their bushes.

"Yes, quite a crowd," Maggie agreed. "A lot of Kansas City's hotshots are here. You know, the big donors."

"Are you a patron?"

"Hardly. Not that I don't appreciate fine art," Maggie quickly added. "Actually, Sarah's a member of the Friends of Art or something like that. She got the invitation. We're her guests. She and Marshall should be here. Let's circulate and look for them.

Sarah wished she could see Maggie's face. Her guests! How had Maggie managed to get around the doorman?

"I have to see Sarah tonight to finalize some details for the fashion show I'm in charge of at the hospital. Most of those auxiliary women are a little hard to take. Sarah is the go-between." Her voice faded as the couple moved off.

"Whew! That was close," Sarah said.

"Did you invite them to the museum?"

"No, but I'm going to find out how they managed to get in. Maggie asked me what we were doing this evening, and I told her. I wouldn't be surprised if they showed up at the Savoy for dinner."

"Why do you think she wants to be with us?"

"Well, maybe she likes us. You'll have to ask her." Sarah weaseled out of the question. "There's my brother. Come on, I'll introduce you."

Together they walked toward her brother and his wife, depositing their plates on a waiter's tray as he passed. Sarah was glad she had remembered to call Matt at work. He would not disclose her secret.

"Hi, Matt, Jessie." Matt was two years older than Sarah, and they had always been close. His wife, Jessica, had grown up in their neighborhood, had played with them as children, and had carried a torch for Matt since she was fourteen and he was eighteen. But it was only after Matt had graduated from college that he noticed the little brat, who had tagged after him years before, had grown into a real beauty. Six months later, they had married.

Sarah introduced them to Marshall, and the two men shook hands, with Matt openly giving Marshall the once-over.

"In the absence of my father, I feel it's my duty to ask if your intentions toward my sister are honorable," Matt said, a twinkle in his eye.

"Matt Madison!" Sarah was aghast.

"That's a tough question. I do have intentions," Marshall said and slipped his arm around Sarah's waist in a possessive manner.

"Marshall!" Sarah exclaimed.

He grinned down at her. "I think I'm lucky your father's out of town.

"Speaking of Dad," Sarah said to change the subject, "have you heard from him or Mom since they've been gone?"

"Not a word," Matt said.

"Yes, we did, honey," Jessie inserted. "They called this evening while you were in the shower. We were running late, as usual, and I forgot to tell you. Your folks will be back Friday night. We're to pick them up at the airport."

"Ah, Jessie, did you forget we're to meet the Barlows at the lake Friday night?"

Jessie sighed. "I knew there was something, but I couldn't remember what. And we were so hurried tonight, it didn't even register that we'd already made plans."

"I'm free Friday night. I'll pick them up," Sarah offered. "Which airline? What time?"

Jessie gave her the details.

"What do you think of the exhibit?" Sarah asked.

"We haven't seen it yet," Matt answered. "We headed straight for the hors d'oeuvres. Lead the way, and we'll take a look."

The foursome wandered back into the exhibit area. Marshall saw Maggie and Jason first and steered his group to the opposite end of the huge room. Sarah and Marshall exchanged conspiratorial glances since Matt and Jessie did not realize they had been maneuvered across the room for a reason.

Marshall kept them moving until they paused too long in front of Sarah's favorite portrait of the girl at the piano.

"Sarah, Marshall," Maggie called out and covered the few yards separating them. "Hi, Matt. Hi, Jessie. How do you like the exhibit?" She gave Sarah a look that said, "I'm here, so make the best of it."

Sarah was sorely challenged not to be rude to her friend. This capped her day, but she smiled and admitted to herself that she had been beaten at the little game of hide-and-seek that they had been playing.

"Maggie, what a surprise to see you here." She could at least make Maggie squirm a little in front of Jason.

"I changed my mind about your invitation," Maggie said quickly. After Jason was introduced to the Madisons, she said, "Would you excuse us a minute. I need to discuss with Sarah a few things that I know would bore you." She took Sarah's arm and led her over to the viewing bench near the center of the room.

"How did you get in? Bribe the doorman?"

"Now, Sarah, don't get huffy. This seemed like such an uptown thing to do. Besides, I like dressing up."

"I'm still curious. How did you get in?"

"Simple. I told the doorman that we were your guests and that we were to meet you here since you'd been delayed at the hospital again. We were here when the door opened. I was hoping you'd be late, as usual."

"We were probably ten minutes behind you, maybe fifteen," Sarah admitted. "So, what are your plans for the rest of the evening?"

"We're going out to dinner."

"Let me guess where," Sarah said sarcastically.

"Well, face it, Sarah. How many places are there where we'd fit right in wearing formal dress? I didn't think you'd mind."

"Do you have reservations? It may be hard to get in without them."

"I had them change Marshall's request to a table for four."

"Maggie! I've got to hand it to you. You've got nerve. But tonight it might work out for the best. I've been snapping at Marshall, and another couple as a buffer may be what we need. But tomorrow night, don't come near us," Sarah warned.

"Not to worry. I have a fashion show at the Woman's Club, so I won't even be seeing Jason. Let's go back to the guys."

❧

Maggie and Jason had taken a cab to the museum, so they rode to the restaurant with Sarah and Marshall. Once inside the elegant old building, Marshall asked the maitre d' if his reservation for two could be changed to accommodate four.

Sarah exchanged a smug glance with Maggie, but the maitre d' was too well-mannered to tell Marshall that the change had already been made, and without comment he escorted them to their table in a corner.

"Isn't this cozy? Boy, girl, boy, girl," Maggie said.

No one commented, but studied their menus. After they had ordered, Marshall said, "Nice place. Do you come here often.

"On special occasions," Sarah answered. "My sixteenth birthday comes to mind. My boyfriend and my family came. I was embarrassed the entire evening. My brothers teased me unmercifully."

"I can believe that after meeting Matt tonight. Is Joe like him?"

"Worse. He teases in two languages."

"Joe is definitely worse," Maggie chimed in. "Remember that time we doubled and our dates took us back to your house since I was spending the night? Matt and Joe were home from college, and they met us outside the door. Wouldn't even let our dates say good night properly." Maggie laughed. "Those guys were so overprotective, they were a pain."

"I think I like your brothers," Marshall said.

"They're not overprotective now. Matter of fact, Matt

and Jessie are always matchmaking. Luckily, Joe and Robin live too far away to set me up."

They had all ordered seafood, which was flown up from the Gulf daily, and as soon as the waiter set their plates in front of them, conversation dwindled for a few minutes.

"This is yummy. Have you tried some of the different restaurants in town?" Maggie asked the men.

"I ate at a little deli today," Marshall answered. "Good sandwich. We've been here since Monday, and that night we met you. Last night was a hot dog at the park, and tonight this."

"I wondered where you had disappeared for lunch," Jason said. "Uh, Dr. Webster came to the dining room alone and looked a bit put out. I knew you two had been talking earlier." He looked expectantly at Marshall.

Sarah knew from their exchange that Dr. Webster was the woman in pink.

"Kerry was so pushy. I tried politely to get rid of her, but she wouldn't take the hint. I finally had to be rude. Women doctors."

"You don't like women doctors?" Maggie asked with sudden interest, holding her fork halfway to her mouth.

Marshall looked at Sarah. She had objected to his opinion of women doctors earlier that evening, and he should have been smarter than to voice his opinion again.

"Oh, they're just like male doctors, some good, some not so good," he told Maggie.

"Really? For a moment there I thought you had some prejudice against them. You know, the old women-belong-in-the-kitchen routine."

"Oh, no. I believe a woman is as capable as a man."

"What about you, Jason? What's your opinion of women?" Maggie asked.

"I like them. There are basic differences between men and women, and I like that, too," Jason said with a wink.

"Oh, you," Maggie said and laughed. "Excuse us a moment," she said and motioned for Sarah to join her.

"Why do they always go in pairs?" Jason asked his friend.

"So they can talk about us, I imagine. Listen, I thought I'd invite Sarah to go to the banquet Saturday night."

"Me, too. Maggie has to work tomorrow night, but I thought we'd do something Friday night and make the banquet Saturday."

"They might find it boring."

"Not with us as their escorts," Jason said with a laugh.

"We can attend the banquet together, but this is the last double date, my friend," Marshall said.

"Fine with me. I'd like to be alone with Maggie, but she's keeping me at arm's length. I think she's been burned. She's told me a little about her ex, and he sounds like a real jerk. How are things going with Sarah?"

Marshall did not want to answer that question. His relationship with Sarah was nothing he cared to discuss with anyone. He was not even sure what their relationship was.

"I like her," was all he said.

❧

"Have you asked Marshall to the fashion show yet?" Maggie asked as she reapplied her lipstick.

"Not yet. But I will. I went to a convention meeting today and had to hide to avoid him. I want Ellen's money for research, but I'm not sure I know what we're trying to prove with this dare."

Maggie flipped her hair back in a fluffing gesture. "That we have different sides to our personalities than normally show. You're not to be a doctor or intimidate him with your intelligence. And I don't believe taking him to a museum fits that part," she said, turning from the mirror to face Sarah.

"He doesn't know I'm a doctor, but he likes intelligent women."

"Yeah, right," Maggie said as the two women walked back to their table.

Over dessert the conversation turned to the convention, and Marshall asked the women to the banquet.

"Sounds interesting," Maggie said. "Sarah and I were just discussing the fashion show at the hospital. It's at two o'clock Saturday afternoon."

This was her opportunity, Sarah knew. Maggie had set her up so she could do the asking, but would that matter if they both completed their dares? It was important that she win the money for research.

"Would you like to come?" she asked Marshall.

"Hey, I'll go," Jason said. "I'd like to see what you do for a living, Maggie."

"Sure," Marshall agreed. "You can show me around the hospital, Sarah. The closing speaker for the banquet is from there. I was reading the program this morning. Dr. Warner Lewis. Quite distinguished from the bio I read. Have you met him?" He rather doubted that she would have since Lewis was such an esteemed research doctor and probably did not mix with the volunteers.

"Yes. I know him. He's brilliant and quite down-to-earth, an unusual combination."

"Anyone want more coffee?" Marshall asked. No one did. "In that case, Jason, can we drop you somewhere?"

"Take us to Maggie's," he said. "I'll find my way to the hotel from there."

"Oh, well," Maggie began a protest. "It's already late.

Perhaps it would be best if you dropped me off then took Jason to the hotel."

"Too much trouble," Jason said. Sarah could hear them discussing their destination as they walked out to the car.

"Marshall wants to be alone with Sarah," Jason whispered loud enough for Sarah to hear. That thought set her heart beating double-time. She wanted to be alone with him, too.

She caught the wink Jason gave Marshall and laughed to herself. Men were such boys sometimes.

As Marshall drove them to her house, Sarah made a sudden decision. She had intended to return to the hospital as soon as Marshall left her house, but she wanted him to stay a while. She had also promised Andrea that she would see her this evening, and the hour was already late.

"Would you mind if we checked on Andrea?"

"The little girl at the hospital?"

"Yes."

"Give me directions but with plenty of warning before the turns," he added with a chuckle.

She told him all the turns and had him park in the staff parking lot. The eleven-to-seven shift was already on duty, but there were plenty of parking places left. She would not tell him she was a doctor, so she could keep her word to her friends, but he would find out as soon as they entered the hospital. Besides, he had already agreed to attend the fashion show. She would argue the technicality with Ellen and Maggie later, but right now she needed to see a special little girl, perhaps for the last time.

Andrea's room was not far from the elevator. Sarah waved to a couple of nurses at the station, one on the phone and the other counting out medicine. She knew they were both checking out Marshall as they walked down the hall.

Outside Room 202 she paused before quietly opening the door. Mr. and Mrs. Garren sat side by side on the daybed that had been brought in for them. They were holding hands, but not speaking, their gazes focused on their daughter. Andrea lay asleep, her breathing labored.

Sarah glided across the room to them. "How long has she been asleep?" she asked in a hushed tone.

"About two hours. Dr. Lewis came in earlier this evening. He said it could be any time." Mrs. Garren was dry-eyed, but the puffiness around her eyes told that she had been crying.

Sarah laid her hand on Andrea's forehead. She did not need a thermometer to know the child was burning up with fever. Marshall crossed to the bed and felt Andrea's hand. His gaze met Sarah's and she nodded.

"Mr. and Mrs. Garren, this is Dr. Adams," she said simply. There was nothing she could do for Andrea and she knew it. "Is there something I can get for you? A cold drink? Have you eaten dinner?"

"We weren't hungry," Mrs. Garren said.

"Nevertheless, I'll have some sandwiches sent up."

"Mama." Andrea stirred. The voices must have disturbed her. Mrs. Garren was at her side instantly. Marshall moved away from the bed to make room for Andrea's father.

"How are you feeling, my little scamp?" Sarah asked.

"Hot. I'm hot," Andrea replied in a week voice. "You look beautiful." Sarah had forgotten she was in her beaded dress. "Where's my Sarah?" the little girl asked.

Mrs. Garren retrieved the doll from the table. "Here you are, darling. I moved her when you were rolling over on her. I'll put her here by Tammy."

Andrea smiled, then closed her eyes again.

Sarah could tell the Garrens needed time alone with their daughter. "I'll see you in the morning."

Mrs. Garren nodded. "Thanks for coming back tonight."

"You're welcome." Sarah took Marshall's hand, and together they walked to the nurses' station.

Marshall felt his fingers cramp with the tight grip Sarah had on his hand. She was hurting, but dealing with it the best she could. He wished some of the volunteers at his hospital showed as much compassion toward patients and especially toward their families.

"Mary," Sarah said to the plump nurse behind the counter. "Would you please see that the Garrens in 202 get sandwiches and cold drinks, in about twenty minutes?"

"I'll take care of it," Mary answered. "You look very nice tonight.

"Thanks." Sarah could tell that Mary wanted an introduction. "I'd like you to meet Dr. Adams. Marshall, this is Mary Hinman, the best night nurse in the hospital."

"That's high praise coming from Sarah," Marshall said. "It's nice to meet you, Mary."

"My pleasure," Mary said, extending her hand to shake Marshall's enthusiastically and nodding to Sarah in approval.

Sarah ushered Marshall out of the hospital, waiting for him to explode about her keeping her profession from him. But he seemed not in the least perturbed and did not mention it.

"What did you think of Andrea?" Sarah asked, wanting to get the subject out in the open.

"You were right; she's dying. Probably tomorrow. All the signs are there. Cancer."

"Leukemia. Acute nonlymphocytic. The odds were against her from the beginning. Experimental treatments haven't worked." What was she doing? She sounded like Hal. It was not her fault that Andrea was dying. Although Sarah knew that was true, she did not want to sound as callous as Hal.

Marshall took her hand, giving her what comfort he could. Sarah's love for the little girl touched his heart. She had studied the doctor's diagnosis and had known all along there was little hope for this type of leukemia. She had probably researched it.

"You should have been a. . . ," he had started to say "nurse," but after his other chauvinistic remarks, he changed it to, "doctor. You care so much about the patients, don't you? I'll bet Andrea isn't an isolated case where you've become attached. Compassion is missing in lots of doctors, and I believe it's essential."

"Thank you, Marshall." Obviously he still did not know. Thinking back over the conversations at the hospital, she realized no one had called her Dr. Madison or Dr. Sarah, as she was known to her small patients.

A comfortable silence lasted until Marshall drove into Sarah's driveway. She had enjoyed having him hold her hand. His touch was not merely sensuous; it was much deeper than that. She felt a special kinship with this man.

Marshall took Sarah's key and opened her front door. He hesitated for a moment, thinking Sarah was not going to issue an invitation, but she must have thought it was understood, because she stepped into the entry and looked over her shoulder as if she expected him to follow. He immediately crossed the threshold.

"Coffee, Marshall?"

"Sounds good." He followed her to the kitchen.

Sarah filled the coffeemaker and puttered around the kitchen, setting coffee cups and saucers on a tray and adding a plate full of cookies she had taken from a tin.

Marshall looked around the kitchen, taking in all the little things he had promised himself he would notice about her house. The room was brightly colored, yellow daisies dominated the wallpaper, and the cabinets were a warm oak. She would probably be like this, warm and sunny in the mornings, puttering around the kitchen, fixing breakfast for him.

What was he thinking? It seemed he always thought of her in terms of the rest of his life, instead of until Sunday when he would leave to go back to Neosho.

"Shall we go into the living room?" Sarah asked, as she poured the coffee.

Marshall picked up the tray and followed her through the entry and into the living room. The lamp still poured its soft light, welcoming them back to the comfortable room. Marshall sat the tray on the coffee table and took his place on the couch beside Sarah. He handed her a cup and took a long drink of his own.

"This is good," he said to make conversation. He felt suddenly shy with this woman. As much as he wanted to hold her, he did not want to make a wrong move and alienate her.

"Thank you," Sarah answered politely. This was the moment she had been waiting for all day. She wanted him to take her in his arms and hold her, kiss her as he had on their two previous dates. Except this time there was not another couple with them or a cab driver waiting. This time they were completely alone.

Marshall studied Sarah over the rim of his cup. Unless his male instincts were wrong, and they were usually very reliable, she wanted him to kiss her. But what if he were wrong? Maybe he was rushing her. No, he was right. He knew he was right.

He set his coffee cup on the saucer with a clatter. He had not meant to use such force. Sarah took another sip, and set hers beside his, a bit more gently. With practiced ease, he put his arm around her and drew her close. She laid her head on his chest, and he could feel the tension ease out of her as he ran his fingers back and forth across the back of her neck. Little Andrea had her tied in knots, but he was going to make her forget, for a little while at least.

Sarah felt as if she had come home. The one place in the world where she belonged was in this man's arms. As he massaged her neck, she relaxed more and more.

"That feels wonderful," she told him. "I've been waiting for this all day." Oh, she hadn't meant to say that. It had slipped out.

"Me, too," he said and turned her in his arms so he could lower his mouth to hers and claim her lips.

His lips caressed hers as his hands slid down her spine and puller her closer. He could not get enough of Sarah. He moved his left hand lower on her back when his cuff link got hooked on the beaded fabric. It took a moment for him to realize what had happened. Reluctantly, he slid his other hand to unhook the cuff link but, as it slid down, it snagged the dress, too.

"Sarah," he whispered, breaking off their kiss. "I'm stuck on you."

Sarah chuckled. "I'll bet you say that to all the girls."

"No, Sarah, I mean it. My cuff link is caught on these beads."

"Really?"

"Yes, really." He tried to wiggle his hands free, but only succeeded in tightening the hold her dress had on him.

"Don't tug, Marshall," Sarah instructed. "If we could

stand up and move toward the light, I think I can get you loose without damaging my dress."

They struggled to stand. In a manner that the Three Stooges would have envied, they inched toward the light. Sarah had an attack of the giggles, which ended in outright laughter.

"I don't see anything funny about this," Marshall growled.

"No, I'm sure you don't," Sarah agreed. "But someday you'll look back on this less-than-romantic moment and laugh."

With his hands locked in place on her back, she wondered that she could see the humor herself, but dissolved into laughter once again when she thought of the ridiculousness of the situation. She took a deep breath, then another to control herself, and set to work.

Carefully, so as not to tear the threads that held the delicate beading, she managed to slip the first cuff link free from the small of her back. Now that he had a free hand, he could help with the one that was higher and impossible for her to reach.

"You'll have to work on this one," she said, turning her back to the lamp so he could get a better view.

She felt his free hand on her waist.

"Are you working on it."

"You bet I am. I'm even beginning to see some humor in this." He continued to move his hand slowly across her back.

"Marshall! Get busy on that cuff link," Sarah ordered.

"Okay, okay." He got it loose, but his hands continued to roam over her back.

Sarah twirled as soon as both hands began to move.

"Marshall!"

He caught her and held her close and kissed her as best he could, for she was choking with laughter again.

"Does this mean the mood is broken?" he asked, looking like a little boy who had just dropped his ice cream cone.

Sarah laughed so hard, tears came to her eyes. She leaned her head against his chest and placed her hands on his broad shoulders.

"You are good for me, Marshall."

"Ah, Sarah, you're good for me." He rested his chin on her head.

They stood like that for a long moment, then Sarah pulled back.

"I think we'd better call it a night, Marshall. It's late, and I'm usually not out every night during the week. I'm beginning to feel the late nights."

"What about tomorrow night? May I see you if we make it an early night?"

"I'd like that. In fact, I'd thought of showing you one more of Kansas City's attractions. The Gaslight Dinner Theater is performing a Neil Simon comedy I thought you might enjoy. But it probably will be just as late a night."

"That's okay. I'll go straight home afterward. Promise. What time should I pick you up?"

"Dinner's at seven, curtain at eight."

"I'll be here. It's not formal, is it?"

"No. A sports coat is fine."

"Good. No more cuff links."

Sarah laughed out loud. Marshall gave her a swift kiss. He put his arm around her shoulders, and she put her arm around his waist as they walked to the front door.

"Good night, Marshall."

"Good night, Sarah." He gave her another kiss, a definite good night kiss, long and lingering and leaving her wanting more.

"I'll see you tomorrow night," he said and with a wave of his hand, he was out the door.

Sarah leaned against the closed door and smiled. Marshall was a wonderful friend. He was more than a friend. If she did not watch it, she could find herself falling in love with this man, if she were not already in love with him. How had this happened so quickly? She tried to picture Jeff in her mind, remember the lesson she had learned from him, but she could not bring his image into focus. Instead, dark hair and the bluest eyes in Missouri crowded Jeff out of her mind.

Marshall certainly knew what to do to make her feel good. He understood her. She could hardly wait until Saturday when she could tell him about her profession and erase that secret from between them. She was still amazed that he had not discovered it for himself at the hospital.

That thought brought Andrea back to mind, and Sarah's up mood took a nose dive. She cleaned up the coffee cups, and as she climbed the stairs to her bedroom, she decided to set her alarm an hour earlier than usual so she could stay with Andrea awhile.

Sarah picked up her Bible from the night stand. It opened automatically to Ecclesiastes 3:1. "There is a time for everything, and a season for every activity under heaven." She knew the passage by heart. She read it whenever she was faced with losing a child. "A time to be born and a time to die." She closed her eyes and prayed.

seven

The days of Indian summer would not last long, and Marshall was determined to be out in that early morning September sunshine. Although he was used to wearing ties, today he chose a short-sleeved plaid shirt and blue jeans.

Marshall was going to play hooky. He wanted to see more of the art gallery and decided to do some shopping at the Plaza, as well. There was also the War Memorial he had seen in a guidebook in his convention packet. He might check that out, too. And the huge old train station had been remodeled into shops and offices. He would like to see that. In short, he was going sightseeing. He would have loved for Sarah to show him around, but since she had to teach today, that was out of the question. Once again he had failed to find out where she taught. Odd, she had never talked about her job or her students. Of course, they had packed every minute pretty full and, at the moment, she was more concerned with Andrea than with teaching health. He knew she would be at the hospital after school and maybe during any free hour she had, so he would send roses to her there. This was one day he was sure she could use cheering up.

He could make the breakfast meeting this morning, but that was it. If he had been smart, he would have skipped yesterday afternoon's session. It was hard to tell which workshops would be good and which would be a waste of time. If he missed an exceptional one today, Ed could fill him in later. He would try to talk Jason into going with him.

Marshall took the stairs at a jogging pace. He needed to be outside getting some exercise; he missed his usual routine. All he had done since he had been in Kansas City was eat and sit. Time for some action as soon as the breakfast meeting was over.

He bought a newspaper from the machine at the front desk and leisurely walked into the dining room. It was still early. The meeting would not start for at least forty-five minutes, plenty of time for him to have coffee and read the paper.

He had made it through the front section, had chatted with an eager waitress, and had picked up the sports section to read about the Royals' chance in the upcoming World Series, when Ed joined him at the round table.

"How's it going, Marshall? How's your latest fling going."

"Fine," Marshall said shortly. He did not want to discuss Sarah with Ed.

"Didn't you take her out last night?" Ed asked. "I went by your room and you weren't there." Since Ed was intent on finding out about his date, Marshall was not going to give it more importance in Ed's eyes by concealing it. He waited until the waitress had poured Ed a cup of coffee before he answered. "We went to the Renoir opening at the art gallery and to dinner afterward. Jason and Maggie went, too."

"You're slipping, Marshall. Double dating didn't used to be your style." Ed laughed.

"It just worked out that way." He was going to say more, but at that moment Hal Mosley stopped by their table.

"Good morning, Dr. Adams. May I join you?"

"Of course." Marshall wondered at Hal's desire to join them. There were any number of tables to choose from and he wished Sarah's friend had picked one of them. Marshall introduced Ed to Hal and the two doctors shook hands.

"So, you and Sarah are old college friends," Hal started the conversation.

"What?" Ed said, obviously startled by that revelation.

"That's right," Marshall said smoothly. "By the way, Mosley, you left your checkbook in my car yesterday when Sarah gave you a ride. She's returning it to your office today."

The waitress had zipped over the moment Hal had sat down and looked him up and down as she poured his coffee.

"Thanks. It was nice of you to lend Sarah your car while hers was in the shop."

"How long have you known Sarah, Dr. Mosley?" Ed asked.

"Sarah and I have been seeing each other for over a year now," Hal explained to Ed, but his gaze was locked on Marshall.

"She's been seeing her old college friend this week," Ed said. "Every night." Ed was obviously enjoying this little show.

"Yes. I'm sure she and Dr. Adams have a lot to catch up on."

"Yes, I'm sure they do," Ed said and laughed.

Marshall had had enough of the inferences. Yet, he was male enough to stake his claim in this conversation.

"Sarah's very upset this morning about Andrea."

"You spoke with her this morning?" Hal asked, then looked as if he regretted his words.

"Yes," Marshall said. Well, it had been after midnight when he had left Sarah and technically that was this morning. Let Mosley draw his own conclusions.

"I know she's upset, but she has to learn that we get the ones who aren't going to survive. She gets too attached to them."

"This one seems special to her. We stopped by and saw her last night, and all the signs were there. I doubt she lasts many more hours."

"Sarah's known this was coming. She should have prepared for it. We talked about it yesterday. I'll have to console her again."

The way he said it told Marshall just exactly how he consoled Sarah. He did not believe it, not for a minute. This pompous man was lying about the woman Marshall loved.

What? He did not love Sarah, did he? He liked her; that much he knew for sure. And he respected her. But love? He had known her for only three days yet he had dreamed about her fixing breakfast for him and showing her the Valley.

Marshall's thoughts kept him silent. He did not know what to reply to Mosley's bomb so he contemplated the bottom of his empty coffee cup.

"Morning, doctors." Marshall looked up to see Jason, standing at their table.

"Morning, Jason. Join us," he said to his friend. He caught the eye of the waitress, which was not hard to do since she kept staring alternately at him and Hal, and motioned for more coffee.

Was Hal Mosley good-looking? He tried to see the doctor through the eyes of a woman and did not like what he saw. The jerk was athletically built and he obviously kept in shape. His blond hair was cut a little shorter than style dictated, but was full and shiny and, the way he combed it, it dipped over one eye. Hal must have felt Marshall's stare for he looked across the table at him. Gray eyes. Steel gray eyes and a firm chin. Since Marshall had not introduced

Jason, Hal took the initiative, stood up, and introduced himself.

Ah-hah. Marshall smiled to himself. He was a good two, maybe three inches taller than Mosley. That should count for something. Of course, that still left Mosley at six foot, two.

The waitress hovered at their table. She poured Marshall another cup and brought a fresh one for Jason. She gave the newcomer the once-over, then returned to Hal and gave him a bright smile.

Okay, Mosley was good-looking but he was still a jerk. Marshall was sure that Mosley's relationship with Sarah was not what he had implied, but was a simple friendship. Well, maybe a bit more than that. She had told him that they went out, but she was obviously not interested in the guy, or why would she be spending every evening with him? And she surely was not going to be consoled by Mosley tonight. If there were any consoling to be done, Marshall would be doing it.

"How was your date last night, Jason?" Ed asked.

Marshall had expected Ed to get to that question. He listened intently for Jason's answer.

"Just fine. That's quite an art gallery you have here, Dr. Mosley."

"Call me Hal. And yes, it's a fine museum, known nationwide for its permanent exhibits. I go there often and rarely miss a traveling exhibit."

"You missed one last night," Ed said slyly.

"Yes. Unfortunately, I was on call at the hospital. And I needed to review the paper I'm presenting this morning."

"Oh. What topic?" Jason asked.

"Heart transplants in infants."

"Doctor Harold Mosley," Ed mused. "Not the eminent Dr. Mosley who performed the Baby John transplant?"

Marshall nearly choked on his coffee.

"One and the same, although I don't know that I consider myself 'eminent,' " Hal said modestly.

"Tell me about the transplant," Ed said eagerly.

Marshall glared across at Ed, the traitor. So Mosley was some hotshot surgeon. He tried to remember what Sarah had called him. Simply a cardiologist. She had not said he was a surgeon. Of course Mosley worked at Children's Research, so he should have put two and two together.

Turning to Jason, Marshall tried to block out the conversation between Ed and Hal. "I'm going to cut the meetings today and see some of the city. Want to come along?"

"Sounds good. But why don't we hear Hal's speech first, then go? His is the first session."

Marshall could not believe that his best friend had turned on him, too. Then he remembered that Jason had arrived after Mosley's comments about Sarah.

"He dates Sarah," he said half under his breath.

"No kidding? An interesting development. At least you know he has good taste," Jason said offhandedly.

"Right." Marshall wanted out of there, away from the wonderful Dr. Mosley. Yet, he would rather have Jason with him than sightsee on his own. He toyed with his coffee cup, deciding what to do.

"Good morning, Marshall," a soft, feminine voice greeted him.

Now what? he wondered. He looked up to Dr. Kerry Webster's hard gaze, then introduced her to Hal.

"Dr. Mosley, I'm looking forward to your talk," Kerry cooed.

Marshall thought he was going to be sick. He had decided to walk out, but the president called the session to order, so Marshall stayed and was herded through the breakfast line with the others.

Kerry managed to sit by Hal. They deserved one another, Marshall thought. Small talk and shoptalk ensued with Marshall contributing monosyllables. As soon as he finished eating, he excused himself.

At the front desk he inquired about a nearby florist and received directions to a shop within walking distance.

The fresh air felt good, and Marshall needed the exercise. He covered the four blocks in record time, ordered the roses for Sarah, and returned in time to see his little breakfast group standing together in the lobby. Kerry was hanging on every word Mosley uttered. Mosley stood tall in his dark, three-piece suit, looking more like a stockbroker than a doctor. Marshall looked down at his own clothes, shirt and jeans, and wondered why he had picked today, of all days, to dress casually.

Jason walked over to him. "Coming to the first meeting? Then we'll go see the sights."

"I'll make some phone calls first, then be along."

He took the stairs two at a time, called his office, and was cheered with the news that his elderly patient was doing better. He walked slowly back down the stairs.

He did not want to go to Mosley's speech, but was drawn there like a moth to a flame. He wanted to see what this guy was like, to see what Sarah saw in him. The door to the meeting room was shut, but Mosley's voice carried into the hall. Marshall slipped inside and saw Jason sitting in the last row with his sports coat draped over the empty seat beside him.

"Thanks," Marshall whispered, as he handed Jason his coat. He settled down in a hostile frame of mind to listen to the eminent Dr. Harold Mosley.

An hour and ten minutes later, Marshall and Jason exited the underground parking lot. Jason sat in the passenger's seat, his hands full of brochures and a map he had taken from the hotel lobby.

"You've got to admit he's a good speaker," Jason said. He had been talking about Mosley since they had climbed in the car, and Marshall was sick of the subject.

"I don't have to admit any such thing," Marshall said belligerently.

"What's gotten into you?" Jason asked. "Oh, Sarah, huh? So what? The man dates Sarah."

"He hinted that they were more than friends."

"Marshall, did you ever consider that they might be? What do you expect of her? She's twenty-nine. Do you think she's been locked in an attic the last ten years?"

"No, I don't. And how do you know how old she is?"

"She and Maggie are the same age."

"Oh," Marshall said and after a couple of minutes of silence, returned to the topic at hand. "Sarah told me there was nothing between them, just an occasional date."

"And you believed her?"

"Of course. She wouldn't lie to me. There would be no reason to. We met him Monday night in the coffeehouse, and she pretty much told him to scram."

"You're dreaming if you think Sarah wouldn't lie to you. She's a woman, isn't she? You can trust me on this one, buddy. Women lie."

"Not Sarah. She's different."

"Right. They're all different," Jason said cynically. He flipped through the brochures he was holding and held one up. "Let's walk around the Plaza first." He found their position on the map. "At the next light, take a left."

❧

Sarah had pushed the alarm off as soon as the shrill sound had begun. Although she had been asleep only a few hours, she was wide awake with the first sound of the buzz. She needed to be with Andrea this morning.

After a quick shower and no breakfast, Sarah left for the hospital. It was not quite six when she walked into Andrea's room.

One look at the little girl's waxy skin and she knew Andrea would not make it through the day. The Garrens were stretched out together on the daybed. Mr. Garren was staring up at the ceiling as he held his sleeping wife close to him. He looked questioningly at Sarah. She motioned for him to stay as he was and not disturb his wife. The woman would need some rest to get her through the day.

Sarah walked to Andrea's side and touched her forehead. Andrea moved her head at the touch. So, she was still conscious. She could slip into a coma any moment now and in a couple of hours it would be all over. Sarah could hardly bear the thought that she would never see those bright, brown eyes again.

Sarah mouthed, "I'll be back," to Mr. Garren and went in search of Mary. She found the night nurse putting the morning medicines in little tablet cups.

"Is there coffee, Mary?"

"Just made a fresh pot. I figured you'd be in before I went off."

Sarah poured herself a cup of the strong brew. She did not have to ask before Mary answered her silent question.

"She's been pretty restless. Up every hour or so. She's been asleep since close to four, the longest nap she's had. That little girl's a fighter. She asked for you once."

"I'll bring the Garrens some coffee and sit with them until time to make the rounds."

Mary gave an understanding smile and nodded in agreement while she poured coffee for the Garrens and set the cups on a small tray.

Balancing the tray, Sarah walked slowly to Room 202. Mrs. Garren was awake when Sarah entered the room. She and her husband were still lying on the daybed, locked in a warm embrace. They were not kissing, just holding and comforting each other.

Mrs. Garren broke away from her husband and sat up on the edge of the bed. He also sat up and took the coffee Sarah offered. "Did you get some rest?" Sarah inquired softly and sat down in the padded, fake-leather chair at the head of Andrea's bed.

"Yes. Andrea was restless most of the night. Much like she was when you dropped in. But the last few hours she's slept and so have I."

"Good."

They all sat in silence for a few moments, their attention focused on the child in the bed. Andrea turned her head, as if feeling their stares, and opened her eyes.

"Dr. Sarah," she whispered. "I don't feel right."

"I know, honey," Sarah answered with a forced smile. "I see you still have your dolls in bed with you. They both have your brown eyes." Sarah was relieved to see the little girl awake again. She had feared Andrea would die before she had the chance to say good-bye. She would not say it out loud to the child, but in her heart, so she could stand this loss more easily.

Sarah moved from the chair so the Garrens could move closer to their daughter. If these moments were important to her, they would be precious to Andrea's parents. They would have to last a lifetime.

"Would you like a cold drink, Andrea? Maybe a Coke?"

"In the morning?" Andrea whispered, a spark of her old self in her eyes.

"I'll make an exception today. Be right back."

Sarah hurried off to get the Coke. She did not usually play waitress to her patients and their parents, but dying days were different. And Andrea deserved a Coke. They had often laughed about having Coke in the morning. Sarah told her she could have it only as an afternoon treat and then again in the early evening. Andrea had attributed drinking Coke as a sign of growing into the teenage years, and now she would never get to experience a first date or the high school prom.

Sarah carried the ice-cold Coke can back into Andrea's room, opened it, and slipped in a straw. She placed the straw in Andrea's mouth and watched as the little girl struggled to sip the cold liquid. She did not have much strength left.

"I've got to make rounds, but I'll be back pretty soon," Sarah told the child. She tried to make her voice sound professional, but it came out too soft for that.

Andrea looked straight into Sarah's eyes as if she were looking into her soul. "Good-bye, Dr. Sarah."

"Good-bye, my little scamp," Sarah said. She bent down and kissed Andrea on her forehead. "I'll see you later."

Sarah walked blindly out of the room. She took a deep breath and then another to gain control.

"Mary," she said as she came to the nurses' station. "Andrea knows. Her parents chose not to tell her, but I just did."

"Dr. Madison," Mary said with a mixture of surprise and concern, "what did you say?"

"I asked her if she wanted a Coke in the morning. It was a joke between us. She always had one as an afternoon treat, something to look forward to."

"She probably already knew," Mary said in sympathy.

"Maybe," Sarah answered. "She didn't seem distraught." She took a deep breath. "I'm going to make early rounds this morning so I can get to the lab and then back to Andrea. Where's Lorraine?" she asked about the nurse who usually accompanied her on rounds, then immediately understood her mistake. "Of course she's not here if you're here, Mary." She glanced at her watch. Fifteen minutes till seven. "I'll start alone. When she comes in, have her join me."

Sarah went from room to room, checking on her patients. The normalcy of routine settled around her until she checked the chart of Joey Garrison. The blood count was all wrong. The experimental treatments were not controlling the leukemia. With no further evidence, no proof at all, she knew without a doubt that Joey would be the next Andrea on the list. Her heart broke. She faked a smile, patted Joey on the foot, and told him she thought she heard the breakfast cart coming down the hall.

"I'll be back pretty soon and we'll talk," she said and made a hasty exit.

Sarah had finished her afternoon rounds and was in the leukemia lab again with Dr. Lewis. She had checked on Andrea four more times and the little girl was holding her own, in and out of a light sleep. Sarah had not told Dr. Lewis about her slip with Andrea. She did not know how to broach the subject. The Garrens had said nothing about it and acted as if nothing was different. Maybe she had imagined Andrea's response.

"I'm going down to check on 202," Sarah said offhandedly, in an effort to make her frequent trips seem normal.

Dr. Lewis was not fooled. "Andrea's special, isn't she?"

Sarah studied the brilliant doctor. He had heart. He was not a research scientist lost in another world, but a truly caring person.

"Andrea's special," she agreed. "I'll be right back."

"Wait. I'll go with you," the older man said. He took off his plastic gloves and walked with her down the wide corridor.

They had just reached the door to Andrea's room when

the call light above the door lit up. Exchanging a lightning-quick glance, they rushed into the room to find Mrs. Garren leaning over Andrea and Mr. Garren shouting into the intercom.

Sarah moved quickly beside Mrs. Garren. She heard the death rattle in Andrea's breathing and when Mrs. Garren started to move back to give her more room, she stopped her.

"Stay with her. Hold her hand." Mr. Garren, on the opposite side of the bed, took his daughter's other hand in his large one and held it up by his cheek.

Within two minutes it was over. Sarah watched the little girl gasp for breath and then give up the struggle. Automatically she glanced at her watch. 3:42. She had to force herself not to call for the respirator, but the Garrens had made the decision not to prolong the inevitable and to let Andrea die in peace.

The parents, two doctors, and the nurse who had answered the call, stood in silence for a moment. Sarah knew she should move in and listen for the heartbeat that she would not be able to find, but she could not move. To do so would be to announce to the Garrens that their daughter was gone. She felt Dr. Lewis's gaze on her, and she looked back at him with tear-filled eyes.

Dr. Lewis was the one to step forward and try to find a heartbeat, signifying the end.

"I'm sorry," he said to Andrea's parents.

The anguished sob from Mrs. Garren and the answering one from her husband, tore at Sarah's heart. She could not stop the tears that rolled freely down her cheeks.

Dr. Lewis stepped back from the bed and walked over to Sarah. Mr. Garren moved to his wife's side. They stood with their arms around each other, staring at their dead child.

"Can you take care of them?" Dr. Lewis asked Sarah in a hushed tone.

"Yes," Sarah whispered. Dr. Lewis patted her on the arm and left the room, taking the nurse with him.

Sarah let the Garrens cry for a few minutes while she gained control herself. In the best professional manner she could muster at the moment, she stepped to the intercom and called the nurse back in.

"We have things to do," she said in a choked voice to the Garrens. "First, is there someone I can call who can drive you home? A relative or a friend?"

Mr. Garren gave her a name just as the nurse walked in, and Sarah instructed her to make that call and another to the funeral home the Garrens had chosen.

She wanted to get the parents out of the room, but they were not ready to leave their little girl. Instead, she helped Mrs. Garren gather up Andrea's things. There were her clothes, several pairs of pajamas, coloring books and crayons, a deck of Old Maid cards, and Andrea's two dolls.

Mrs. Garren held out the newer doll to Sarah. "Dr. Madison, she would want you to have the doll she named after you."

Sarah felt the tears forming and blinked them back. She could not start crying again. The Garrens were over their first bout of tears and were in the numbed, shocked period when everything seemed like a bad dream. She did not want them feeling again until they were safely home.

"I will treasure this always," she told Andrea's mother, as she took the doll.

She had to get the Garrens out of the room. The hearse would be there soon, and they did not need to see it take their daughter away.

Sarah ushered the parents into a private waiting room and stayed until their friend arrived. She walked them to the main door, listening to the friend talk about getting the Garren's car later. The Garrens wore blank expressions and looked at the friend as if their car were the last thing in the world that mattered.

At the door, Mrs. Garren turned to Sarah. "Dr. Madison, thank you for caring about our little girl. She loved you, too." She hugged Sarah then walked through the door her husband held for her. He looked back at Sarah and said a quiet thank-you.

She watched them walk out to the car and stood at the door long after the car had disappeared from view.

Cradling the doll in her arms, much as she would have a baby, Sarah walked back to the elevator. She did not wait for it but climbed the stairs and walked quickly to Room 202. Stopping in the doorway, she stared at the housekeeping staff, who were stripping the bed and cleaning the room.

Andrea was already gone.

Sarah stood sightlessly for a moment, looking inward, remembering the bright child who was no more. "God, please take care of her," she whispered.

Then, with a resolute squaring of her shoulders, she turned and walked purposefully toward Joey's room.

eight

Marshall and Jason walked through the lobby from the parking garage.

"I'm beat," Jason said. "Maybe it's a good thing Maggie has to work tonight. Think I'll take a shower, call room service for dinner, and watch a movie in bed. Don't get that sort of luxury very often."

"No, such leisurely nights are few and far between," Marshall agreed. He stopped at the desk and asked if there were any messages for him. He had the feeling Sarah might have called to thank him for the roses.

"Yes, Dr. Adams." The desk clerk handed Marshall a note and flicked a switch that turned off the flashing light on the phone in Marshall's room.

"Well, did she get the flowers?" Jason asked as they walked over to the elevators.

"I don't know," Marshall said, rereading the terse message. "She can't make our date tonight. One of the patients at the hospital where she volunteers must have died. If that's the case, Sarah wouldn't be in the mood for a comedy at the theater."

The elevator arrived, and the two men stepped inside.

"Want to have dinner together?" Jason asked.

"Thanks, but I think I'll order room service, too. Sightseeing is exhausting."

Jason got off on his floor and Marshall rode on to the fifth floor and reread the desk clerk's version of Sarah's message one more time.

Sarah Madison called. She is sorry, but will not be able to make your date tonight.

After a long shower, Marshall stretched out on the bed. He turned on the TV and flicked from one station to another, but nothing held his attention. His thoughts were with Sarah. The note did not say for him to call her back, but nothing kept him from doing it. He should have thought of that before.

The phone rang six times before she answered, and at first he thought he had dialed a wrong number, because her voice sounded so different.

"Sarah, it's Marshall. Is it over?"

"Yes," Sarah said in a low voice. "She died at 3:42. I'd just walked in the room, and a couple of minutes later she was gone." Her voice cracked.

"I'm sorry, Sarah," Marshall said softly.

There was a long silence on Sarah's end, then in a muffled voice she said, "I can't talk now, Marshall. I'm sorry about tonight. Good-bye."

Marshall lowered the phone after he heard the click. That conversation had not gone at all as he had planned. He prowled the room and finally decided to go downstairs for something to eat.

He did not feel like sitting down at a table in the hotel restaurant. A couple of tacos sounded better. With that decision made, he took the elevator to the garage. He felt as if he had walked over half of Kansas City and he did not need the exercise the stairs offered.

The fast-food Mexican place he had remembered seeing was a short drive away. He carried his food to a table by the window and stared out as he ate. What would Sarah be having for supper? Why wouldn't she talk to him? Was it because she was too upset? Or was it because there was someone else there? His mind flew back to the morning conversation with Hal Mosley. Was he there with her now, consoling her? Marshall stuffed the paper trash from his meal into a huge garbage can and stalked out to his car. He started the engine, but instead of turning back toward the hotel, he went in the opposite direction. He told himself it was stupid, that he was acting like a teenager with a crush but, nevertheless, he drove over to Sarah's house.

There were no lights on and no car parked in front of her house. Marshall slowed down but had to drive on past it because of a car tailgating him. He swung around the block and made another pass in front of Sarah's house. Of course, her car would be in her garage, but surely Mosley's would be visible if he were there. There were no lights to be seen from this angle, either, but it was not dark yet. What was she doing in there? Determined to find out even if he made a fool out of himself, he parked and walked to the front door. He rang the bell, but there was no answer. Trying the knob, he was surprised to find it unlocked. He stood uncertainly on the porch with his hand on the doorknob, then opened the door and stuck his head inside.

"Sarah," he called into the empty hall.

He thought he heard a noise and closed the door behind him before walking from the entrance to the living room. The draperies were closed, allowing none of the last rays of the sun into the room. In the dimness he made out Sarah, huddled on the couch.

"Sarah?" he said softly. "Are you all right?"

"Marshall?" she said and sniffed.

"Yes." He reached for the light switch on the lamp, and the room filled with soft light. Sarah blinked. Her eyes were red rimmed, and it took no detective's mind to see that she had been crying.

Marshall walked swiftly across the room and sat down beside her. Without hesitation she moved into his arms, her head resting on his wide chest. She cried; huge, wrenching sobs shook her slender frame. Marshall murmured soft reassuring words and held her close. When the crying subsided, he handed her his handkerchief, then stood and pulled her to her feet.

"We're going for a walk," he said, his voice brooking no argument.

He led her out the front door and walked with his arm around her down the street toward a wooded park area she had pointed out to him before.

"When one of my patients dies," he said, "I always go for a walk in the hills to remind myself of all of God's nature around me. I see His hand in every flower and every leaf. And I see His plan of spring and renewal and fall and quietus."

" 'To everything there is a season,' " Sarah whispered.

"Exactly. Death is the natural result of living, and we shouldn't fear it but rejoice that God has promised an even better life than the one on earth. That doesn't mean I don't grieve for the one who's died, but I'm really grieving because of the void left in my life by the person's death. Am I making any sense?"

She nodded and he continued.

"Everyone has his own way of dealing with death. Mine is to walk. I think of the person who's died, all the good things I knew about that person, characteristics I liked and that I should imitate."

They had reached the park, and Marshall paused to read the wooden sign that declared the area a nature haven in memory of Millie Rawlings.

"What a wonderful monument to a person." He led Sarah through the woods. Many of the leaves had already changed colors, announcing that autumn would end soon and winter begin. But spring would follow. The changing of seasons, as old as time, would still go on.

They walked the length of the park in silence and turned to retrace their steps. Dusk had settled, the western sky painted pink and orange by the setting sun. Within minutes the color would disappear and darkness would fall.

Marshall hurried their pace so they could reach Sarah's home before the light was gone. At home he liked walking after dark, but he did not know these woods or the slope of the land.

When they reached the sidewalk on Sarah's street, he slowed their steps. They had their arms around each other as they walked.

"What did you like about Andrea?" he asked softly.

She was silent a moment. "Her bright eyes, her sunny disposition. I know she's with God now, and I do rejoice in that for her. And I've been thinking back over the times she's been in the hospital. She knew she was dying, Marshall. She knew all along. Her parents couldn't bring themselves to tell her, but she knew, and she wasn't afraid. She was sharp. She watched what went on around her, and she sorted it out for herself. That was why she didn't seem distraught when I told her she could have a Coke this morning. It told her that today was her last day, but she knew that."

"Wait a minute. You've lost me. What about a Coke?"

As Sarah explained about her early morning visit, she withdrew her arm from around him and began wringing her hands together.

Marshall understood. She felt she had betrayed Andrea

somehow. It was his experience that patients knew if they had an incurable disease. Parents were fooling themselves if they thought their children could not read their moods and see their fear and agony and correctly interpret it.

It must have been a horrible day for Sarah. To have the guilt she had laid on herself for the Coke episode and then to go to the hospital after school and arrive just as Andrea died would be a lot to handle. He doubted that Sarah had ever been with anyone else who had died. And to have her first time be with a special little girl must have been heart-breaking.

"Have you had anything to eat?" he asked as soon as they walked back into Sarah's house. At the negative shake of her head, he pushed her in the direction of the kitchen.

"I'll fix you a gourmet meal," he said. "Point me in the direction of the canned goods."

Sarah smiled, the first smile he had seen all evening, and pointed to a door.

Marshall found a well-stocked pantry, but decided she would eat only a little, so chose a can of chicken noodle soup. While it heated on the stove, he checked the refriger-ator and found two French rolls. He sliced them in half, spread them with butter, and sprinkled Parmesan cheese on top before sticking them in the oven under the broiler. He poured two glasses of iced tea, ladled up the soup, and placed the toasted bread in a basket he found on the counter.

"Your dinner is served," he said with a flourish.

Together they sat down at the round kitchen table.

"It looks delicious," Sarah said and started on her soup. Marshall watched her eat and helped himself to a couple of slices of bread. She finished the bowl of soup, but declined a refill. While she sipped her tea and munched on bread, Marshall cleaned up the kitchen.

"Shall we take our tea to the living room?" he suggested.

She nodded. She had smiled a couple of times, had made small talk over supper, but she was not her old self yet. She still needed to talk, to get her grief out in the open.

She sat on the couch, and Marshall walked over to the fireplace. Inside it, wood was laid up for a fire. It was not cold and they did not need a fire for warmth, but the crackling sound and the glow of the flames would lend a cheery atmosphere to the room.

"Do you mind if we have a fire?" She shook her head. "I like fires," he said as he struck a long match from the holder on the mantel and turned on the gas starter. He watched it until the kindling caught, then turned off the gas.

Time to get Sarah talked out, he decided, as he sat down beside her. He placed his arm along the back of the couch, his hand resting on her shoulder.

"How did Andrea's parents handle it?"

"As well as could be expected. She is, was, their only child." The way she said that, as if they would suffer this only once, while she suffered over and over, gave Marshall sudden insight into Sarah's deep depression. She was not grieving for Andrea alone, but for all the children she had known who had died.

"You see a lot of children die at the hospital." It was not a question, just a statement, but she nodded in response.

"The next one will be Joey. He's the same age as Andrea. The one before Andrea was Eric. The one before that was Taryn. It goes on and on. It never stops."

"Perhaps you should consider quitting at the hospital.

Find another hospital for your work, but not one strictly for children. Death is hard to accept any time, but when it strikes children repeatedly, it's especially hard." He felt sure she would be welcomed at any hospital where she chose to volunteer her time.

"You might have something there," she said thoughtfully.

"You know the Serenity Prayer, Sarah?" He did not wait for an answer, but began and Sarah's voice joined his. "God, give us grace to accept with serenity the things that cannot be changed, courage to change the things which should be changed, and the wisdom to distinguish the one from the other."

"Amen," Sarah said and felt a peace settle over her. They sat in silence for a moment, then Sarah said, "Oh, thank you for the flowers, Marshall. I appreciate them." She gazed across the room at the vase of roses on a side table. Marshall had failed to notice them until now.

"I'm glad you like them. The night we met, you left your rose in the cab, and I've been enjoying it in my room." He had not meant to say that, to tell her he prized anything that reminded him of her, but she did not have the triumphant look of a woman with the upper hand. She must not have read the correct meaning into his remark.

"I like it when you hold me," Sarah said softly, catching him off guard. He immediately settled his arms around her and she snuggled to fit her soft curves against his hard frame.

"I like it, too," Marshall murmured into her hair. He understood her need. He had experienced it many times himself. Being close, touching someone, renewed the sense of being alive. And after losing someone, it was necessary to have that feeling. They sat that way for a long time.

Finally, Marshall turned her so he could kiss her lightly on the forehead. It was all he meant to do, but a couple of kisses there led to a kiss on each eye and then to the tip of her nose and her cheek, and then her lips beckoned him. He kissed her again and again.

Sarah nestled closer to him. He knew she was vulnerable tonight, and he did not want to take advantage of that situation. He needed to go. He needed to go because he loved her. And he knew she loved him. He felt it in his heart.

"May I see you tomorrow night?" he asked.

"I'm picking up my parents at the airport tomorrow night. Remember? And this evening I talked to Mom, and she asked me to spend the night out at Lake Quivera with them."

"Could I go to the airport with you? I want to meet your folks."

"That's a new twist," she said. "Most guys shy away from the meet-the-parents routine. Be here at seven."

Marshall grinned again. "Seven." He pulled her into his arms and held her close. He did not want to let her go, and she would never understand what it cost him to leave her. He gave her a quick peck on the cheek and walked out of the house.

He loved her, his heart sang. He had found the woman of his dreams. A warm, loving, intelligent, sensitive Christian woman. She would say yes when he asked her. And she would love the Valley as much as he did. Sarah Madison Adams. Sarah Adams. Dr. and Mrs. Marshall Adams. He liked the sound of that.

nine

"So, you've both got the men coming to the fashion show tomorrow," Ellen said. She sat in the doctors' dining room with Sarah and Maggie. "Sarah hasn't told him she's a doctor, but she sure hasn't played down her intelligence," Maggie said. "She took him to the museum, if you can believe that."

Ellen turned to Sarah, her eyebrows raised in a silent question.

"He likes intelligent women. He told me the first night we met. And I also took him to a baseball game."

"And what a game." Maggie took over the conversation and told Ellen about the mix-up with the box seat tickets and the four of them standing the entire game.

"The fans were on their feet most of the game anyway. And the men did enjoy it," Sarah inserted.

"And the museum?" Ellen asked. "Kent and I attended, but we couldn't make it until late. I'm sorry we missed you."

"Maggie failed to mention that she and Jason crashed that museum party and also attached themselves to us for dinner," Sarah said. She looked at her watch. "We'd better finish up. I need to be back in the lab by one-thirty."

Maggie cut another bite from her chicken breast. "How come we haven't ever eaten in here before? I didn't know you had gourmet dining."

"The hospital treats us right. If the doctors used the cafeteria, families would besiege us, and we wouldn't get to eat." She rarely stopped long enough for a complete meal, but today Ellen had insisted they meet before tomorrow's fashion show and having them come to the hospital was easier for Sarah.

"Now," Ellen said, "we've covered Tuesday and Wednesday. What did you do last night?"

"I'm totally innocent," Maggie announced. "I worked. Big show at the Women's Club. What about you, Sarah?"

"One of our little girls died yesterday and I was upset. So, I called Marshall and canceled our date, but he came over anyway. We went for a walk, and he fixed me dinner. He was very understanding about not going to the theater."

"Did you tell him about the little girl? About being a doctor?" Ellen asked, waving her fork at Sarah.

"He doesn't know. He thinks I'm a volunteer. I told him when I met him that I spend a lot of hours here without getting paid. Which is true. I come in lots of times when I'm not required to."

"Hey, we're not questioning that, just making sure you haven't told him you work here," Maggie said.

"I want to tell him. I like him, and I want him to know the truth. I brought him over here late Wednesday night to check on Andrea, but he didn't find out. No one called me Doctor. Guess I'll have to work on the staff and have them show more respect for the title."

"Sarah," Maggie said. "Tomorrow is only a few hours away. Why ruin this little dare by telling him tonight?"

"But both men have agreed to come to the fashion show. Why carry this little charade further?" It seemed to Sarah that the purpose of the dare had been achieved. She had had fun, proved she had a different side to her personality and a balanced life, but now she felt as if she were trapped in a game. She still believed a doctor's life and a family did not mix, but she wanted to be honest with Marshall and be his friend. No, that was not true, a voice inside her said. There was more than friendship at stake here.

"A dare's a dare," Ellen said. "What's a few more hours?" Maggie asked.

"I suppose you're right." Sarah patted her mouth with her napkin. "Did I tell you Marshall sent me a dozen roses yesterday?"

"Well, well. A promising sign. Ellen, do you think this little experiment has changed Sarah?" Maggie asked.

"I think this little experiment has worked a little wonder," Ellen said with a knowing smile.

Sarah studied Ellen. What was she thinking? Ellen had always been able to discern her innermost thoughts. Perhaps she was right on target once again. Sarah had been more relaxed with Marshall than with any other man she had ever known, and that included Jeff. And she felt something special for Marshall that she had never felt for any other man. She respected him.

Maybe this little dare had helped her. If Marshall's not knowing she was a doctor in some way had helped her relax and be a woman with him, then this dare was worth it.

"I've got to run," Sarah said. "Are you two ready?" She could not leave them in the doctors' lounge by themselves.

"Okay. Tomorrow at two," Ellen said. "I'll meet the men you have maneuvered so skillfully. Let's plan on dinner afterward."

"Oh, Ellen, we failed to mention that the two men skillfully maneuvered us. We're going to the convention banquet with them tomorrow night," Maggie said.

Ellen had stood up to leave, but sat down again in a bout of laughter. "Oh, the games we play." She was still laughing when she was able to walk away, leaving Maggie and Sarah staring after her.

❧

"Hey, Marshall. Where were you this morning?" Ed's booming voice was loud enough for three tables around them to hear. Marshall pulled out a chair and sat down at the dining table with Jason and Ed. Here he was again, eating. He had probably gained five pounds this week. He ordered a chef salad, which was promptly placed in front of him.

"Well?" Ed demanded. "Where were you?"

"I went for a walk and went farther than I'd planned. Did I miss something important?"

"No. But this afternoon's session should be good. The drug companies are conducting seminars. I love it when they pay us to listen to their spiels."

Marshall was not surprised. Although he had to have plenty of money now, Ed's past still exerted an influence on him.

"So, what did you do last night?" Jason asked. "I called your room and you weren't in. The TV movie was lousy, so I thought we could check out a theater."

"I went over to Sarah's. She was feeling pretty low and we talked. I fixed a bit of supper for her."

"Then the little girl died?"

"Yes. Yesterday afternoon. Sarah had just walked into the room. Just came in from school, I guess, and she was there when Andrea died. It hit her pretty hard. Although she's in a hospital where they lose a lot of children, I doubt she's witnessed it before."

"Couldn't you console her like Dr. Mosley does?" Ed asked with a sly smile.

"Dr. Mosley insinuated something that isn't true. They

don't have a relationship, just an occasional date."

"Let me guess. She told you that, and you believe her," Ed said. He exchanged a knowing look with Jason, who shrugged his shoulders.

Marshall already knew Jason's opinion, and he did not like having it seconded by Ed.

"Of course, I believe her. She's not the kind of person to lie."

Ed exchanged another look with Jason. "I believe there may be a little more here than I first thought. Are you hung up on her, Marshall?"

He did not want to answer that question. "I've known her only a few days. She's easy to talk to, that's all. She's a good listener and a good person. We might keep in touch after I go back to Neosho." He wanted to do much more than that. He wanted to show her the Valley, show her what his world was like. And he wanted her to love it, too, and be a willing part of it. But he could not confide in Ed and Jason.

"Oh, really?" Ed said.

"Yes, really. It doesn't mean anything," he said. "Just that we like each other's company. What about you, Jason? Going to see Maggie again after we leave Sunday?"

Jason looked a little sheepish. "I thought I'd invite her out to Denver. Maybe take her skiing over Thanksgiving."

"Well, well," Ed said, shaking his head. "So the old Adams charm is still there, and Bradford has some, too. Want to see the Foster charm?"

Ed pulled out his wallet and extracted a picture from the photo section. He handed the picture of a woman to Marshall, who looked at it, then handed it to Jason.

"You sure this picture didn't come with the wallet?" Jason asked.

As if anticipating the question, Ed handed a second picture to Marshall. The same brunette, Ed and two small children smiled at him from the photo. "She's quite a looker, Ed. How did you manage to catch her?" Marshall asked. He passed the picture to Jason, who gave a low wolf whistle.

"I guess you guys underestimate the Foster charm. And I am true blue to my woman."

Marshall studied his friend. Here was another side to the brash, loud, obnoxious man that he had not suspected. Ed's tone of voice even softened when he spoke of his wife.

"Needra's a wonderful wife and a good mother, too. She doesn't work," he told them, pride in his voice. "She stays home with the children. It was my lucky day when I met her."

"Your chauvinism is showing," Jason said.

"I don't care. My mother had to work, and I swore my wife would never have to. And she doesn't. Her job is to take care of me and our children."

That sounded wonderful to Marshall. What would it be like to go home at night to a warm house filled with the sounds of children's laughter and the smells of dinner cooking on the stove? And be greeted by Sarah at the door, a kiss on her lips just for him. Oh! He was at it again. His visions of the future always included Sarah.

"What are you doing tonight, Marshall?"

"What?" He had heard his name, but not the question. Jason repeated it.

He did not want to answer. He did not want to tell them he was going with Sarah to get her parents at the airport. That would open up more speculation.

"We're going for a drive," he said without mentioning

the destination. He gulped down his last bite of salad and stood up to leave the dining room.

"Going with us this afternoon?" Jason asked.

"No. I need to call my office again, then I might run over to Children's Research to look around a big city hospital. It's been quite a while since our Chicago days, and I'd like to examine the differences, now that I've had experience in a small town."

"We'll be in the Cedar Room, if you change your mind," Jason said.

Marshall nodded and wound his way around the other tables and out into the lobby area. He climbed the stairs to his room and made his phone call, then wandered over to the windows looking down on the city street.

He had enjoyed his walk this morning. He had not intended to miss the morning meeting, but it was such a nice day to be outdoors. He had come to this conference with high hopes of being inspired to be a better doctor, to learn new techniques and procedures, and now he had skipped a day and a half of meetings. Perhaps he should go this afternoon, but these sessions were just live commercials.

On the other hand, the convention planners had scheduled alternative activities for the doctors. Golfing, boating, tours of Kansas City were all listed in the conference guide. All work and no play was not the rule for this convention.

If he went to the hospital, he might run into Sarah. He hoped he would see her as soon as her school day ended. But today she might not volunteer; she might not want to go back to the hospital just yet. Andrea's death was too fresh in her mind. A couple of days away would help her deal with things without so much emotional involvement.

Sarah, he thought. "Sarah," he said aloud. He would see her at seven o'clock. He remembered her sister-in-law telling Sarah that the plane landed at seven-fifty, which would not give them time for dinner. He called Sarah's house and left a message on her machine. He could come over earlier, and they could get a bite to eat before picking up her parents. He hoped she would call him back when she got home from school.

❧

Sarah punched the button on her machine as soon as she arrived home at five-thirty. It had been a rough week, and Dr. Lewis had insisted she leave on time for once. As soon as she heard Marshall's message, she called the hotel.

"Come on over," she told him. "We can pick up something to eat on our way to the airport."

Under the soothing spray of the shower, Sarah thought of Marshall's kindness last night. She had cried in front of him and responded to his kisses. Now she felt shy about seeing him again and at the same time impatient that it would be a half-hour before he could get there.

She showered longer than she had meant to, and then everything went wrong. Mascara caked on her lashes. She took it off twice before she was satisfied with the result. Then she smeared her lipstick. She tried on three outfits and discarded them in favor of a pair of peach-colored slacks and a white blouse. Since the day she had discovered Jeff was seeing other women, she had insulated herself from hurt. Now she realized she had also insulated herself from other feelings, as well. Her profession had helped. She blamed it on men not liking intelligent women. But time had healed the pain, and now she was ready for an emotional involvement—if it worked out that way. She changed clothes one more time and dashed in designer jeans and a sweater to the front door as the bell rang. She opened the door, and Marshall wasted no time in taking her in his arms and kissing her thoroughly.

"Are you all right?" he asked.

"I'm okay," she said. "I'll be just a minute. I need to stick a toothbrush and some pajamas in a bag. It's been a long time since I stayed at my folks'. Oh, Marshall, I just thought, we need to drive to Lake Quivera, so I can get Dad's car. Mine won't hold us."

"I'll drive," he offered.

"But I'll need my car to get back tomorrow. Would you follow me out there?"

❧

The drive to the Kansas side of the state line took longer than she had planned. Sarah locked her car on her parents' driveway and jumped in the car with Marshall.

"Did I tell you Jason and I went sightseeing yesterday?" Marshall asked.

"Really? You skipped meetings?"

"Yes. Well, we heard the esteemed heart specialist talk," he said, trying to keep the sarcasm out of his voice, but failing.

"How did Hal do?" She had meant to go hear him, but was glad she had not taken the time. She had heard him before.

"Fine. I imagine he's used to public speaking."

"He's had a lot of press lately. The Baby John transplant."

"Yes, I know. Hal had breakfast with me yesterday. I'm not his favorite person."

"Oh. Because of me?"

"Yes, dear, because of you." She seemed to digest that piece of information. Marshall did not think she knew how much Hal wanted her for his own. But enough of that. He did not want her thinking of Hal when he was with her. "I skipped this morning's meetings, too. This afternoon I thought I'd tour Children's Research, but I got sidetracked." He had been on his way out of the hotel when he had met another doctor from old school days, and they had renewed their acquaintance over coffee. He glanced over at Sarah and saw her take a deep breath. "Are you all right?" he asked.

"Fine," she said. What if he had walked in on her at the hospital? She needed to tell him about her job herself, in her own way, and explain the importance of the dare and the money for research. "Tomorrow after the fashion show, I'll show you around if you'd like." Then they would laugh about her deception and wonder that he had not found out from Hal or their earlier visit to the hospital.

After a hamburger stop, they arrived at the airport with only five minutes to spare. They rushed to the gate to find the flight was a few minutes behind schedule.

"So, tell me about your parents. Will your dad quiz me like your brother did?" Marshall asked as they settled in chairs for the wait.

"No. My brothers are much more forward than my dad. Mom might ask a few questions."

"Oh, no. Moms are worse than dads."

"Don't panic. I'm just teasing. My mom's a real lady. She won't quiz you about personal things. She's kind, getting more gray hair than she cares to have, and is a bundle of energy. Annie and I could never keep up with her. Now, Dad is sixty-six. He retired two years ago because his hands were beginning to bother him. Arthritis. They moved to Lake Quivera so he could play golf every day and keep his hands in shape. He was a brilliant heart surgeon, but the moment his hands started to go, he turned in his knife. Sometimes he teaches a seminar, or is a guest lecturer, that sort of thing, so he keeps up on what's new in O.R. I think he's content with his new life. He doesn't look back, just keeps looking forward."

At the roar from outside, Sarah peered through the windows at the lights of an approaching plane.

"They're on the ground," she said and glanced at her watch. Only ten minutes had passed. Sarah called to her parents as they walked out of the unloading tunnel.

"Hello, Sarah," her mother said, and they hugged each other.

"Hi, Dad." Sarah kissed her father on the cheek, then introduced Marshall.

They discussed the weather and the flight and Annie's new baby while they waited for the luggage to arrive. As soon as it started down the chute and filled the carousel, Marshall and Dr. Madison picked up the cases Caroline Madison pointed out.

"If you'd like to wait here, I'll get the car," Marshall suggested.

"If it's not far, we can carry the luggage," Dr. Madison said.

Marshall gazed at the two biggest pieces, but assured Sarah's father that it was not far. He started to pick up the two large cases when Dr. Madison stopped him.

"I'll get those, young man," he said and would not hear of Marshall carrying them. Obligingly, Marshall picked up the two smaller cases and led the way to the exit and outside to the car.

"What's he doing?" Sarah whispered to her mother.

"I believe your father is proving in typical male fashion that he's as fit as your young suitor. He feels threatened. His daughter turns up at the airport with a boyfriend who is obviously possessive of her."

"Mom, how can you tell that? We've only talked about the weather."

"Sarah, we've seen three other children go through this. And we were young once ourselves, you know. Besides, it's not in the conversation; it's in the looks and the way he had his arm around your shoulder."

Sarah stared at her mother. She had a keen sense of reading people. "He is special," she said softly.

Her mother smiled and nodded. The men had arrived at the car ahead of them, and Marshall already had the trunk open. Sarah climbed in the front seat and left the backseat for her parents.

On the drive home Caroline Madison asked how Marshall met Sarah, and then they discussed his hometown.

Sarah led the discussion to the fashion show the next day. She had not warned her folks not to mention she was a doctor, and she directed the conversation away from medicine. But as they crossed the bridge over Lake Quivera, her dad asked how things were at the hospital.

"It's been a trying week," Sarah admitted. She turned around in her seat so she could see her father better. He and her mother were sitting close together. "Did Mom tell you we lost a little girl yesterday?"

"Yes. How did you deal with it?"

"Not very well. Marshall took me for a walk, and it helped."

Her dad studied the back of Marshall's head, and Sarah suffered an uncomfortable moment. She had never seen her father like this before.

"I used to walk when I'd lose one," he said finally, a note of respect slipping into his voice. "What's your specialty, Marshall?"

"General practioner. Although, since I practice in a small

town, I'm really more of a family doctor." Marshall met Dr. Madison's gaze in the rearview mirror. Some of the initial hostility he had sensed from Sarah's father was beginning to vanish. Nevertheless, he breathed a sigh of relief when the house came into view. He parked beside Sarah's little sports car, jumped out, and lifted the suitcases out of the trunk before Dr. Madison could climb out of the car.

"Can you come in for a while, Marshall?" Caroline asked.

He glanced at Sarah. "For a few minutes," he said, but wished he was back at the hotel that moment. As they walked to the house, Marshall carried one of the large bags and one of the smaller ones. Dr. Madison's load equaled his.

Marshall set his load down in the entry.

"Could I speak to you a moment?" Dr. Madison asked in a quiet but determined voice.

"Of course," Marshall agreed. He glanced at Sarah, who gave a small shrug, then he followed Dr. Madison into the kitchen.

"Now what's he doing?" Sarah asked in a low voice.

"I don't know, dear. Being with Annie has been hard on him. He wasn't expecting a C-section and seeing her in so much pain brought out all his fatherly instincts. My guess is he's still feeling protective." In the ensuing silence, Sarah could hear a low mumble of voices, but could not make out any words.

In the kitchen, Dr. Madison stood clutching the back of a kitchen chair. "This may be very premature, and I never thought I'd ever say this, but what are your intentions toward my daughter?"

Marshall held the doctor's gaze and answered in a straightforward fashion. "I've known Sarah only since Monday, but in that short time, I've grown to love her. I haven't asked her, and I'd appreciate it if you didn't mention it, but I intend to marry her, if she'll have me. I know that sounds sudden, but that's the truth."

Dr. Madison seemed to relax a little, but stood silent as if taking it all in. "I knew the first time I met Caroline that she was the one for me," he said softly. "But you may be fighting an uphill battle with Sarah. Her work at the hospital is very important to her."

"I know, but she could work at the hospital in Neosho. She's been around dying children so long, she may welcome the chance to see them get well." He believed it would be better for her, and he had given Sarah's job some thought as well. She would want to finish the school year in Kansas City. An eight-month engagement was longer than he wanted, but he could stand it if he knew she would be his wife in June.

"Marshall, forgive me for overstepping the line as Sarah's father. Her sister's just gone through a trying time, and it's hard on an old man to see his daughter in pain. I just want to protect Sarah from hurt."

Marshall smiled. "I understand, Dr. Madison. Sarah was wrong about you. She said Matt was a much tougher inquisitor than you, and she was wrong."

"Oh, when did you meet Matt?"

Marshall explained about the museum exhibit and then told Sarah's father about the baseball game and the mix-up with the tickets.

In the great room, Sarah was wringing her hands together. What were they talking about in there? If her father was grilling Marshall, she should go in and break it up.

A burst of laughter came from the kitchen. Sarah's gaze darted to her mother. A moment later, the two men joined them.

"Walk me to the car?" Marshall asked Sarah.

"Of course," she said.

Her parents shook hands with Marshall, and then the young couple walked outside.

As soon as the door shut behind them, Sarah asked, "What did he want? I've never known my dad to act like that."

"Just man talk," Marshall said with a smile.

"You're not going to tell me?"

"No."

"You're really not going to tell me?" Sarah was amazed.

"No."

"You go in the kitchen with my father, and the hostility could be cut with a knife, and you come out ten minutes later laughing and patting each other on the back. And you're not going to tell me?"

"That's right. Oh, maybe someday I'll let you in on it, but not now."

"Could you at least tell me what you were laughing about?"

"That baseball game we went to."

"That's it?"

"Yes. Now, kiss me good night, then you can enjoy your evening with your folks." But he could not let her go after one kiss. Two and then three melted into four and five.

"I should go back in," Sarah said when he released her mouth for a brief moment.

"I know," he said then hugged her closely.

"I'll see you tomorrow," she whispered in his ear. "Remember, the fashion show at two."

"I'll be there," he promised, then he kissed her once again.

ten

"Maggie, where do you want the microphone?" Sarah called. She was standing beside the maintenance man who was waiting impatiently for the redhead's answer.

"Put it by the entrance door," Maggie called across the large cafeteria. Late-lunch diners turned their heads to watch the action.

The fashion show would start in an hour, and all the last-minute details had yet to be attended to.

"Dr. Madison," a volunteer asked, "do you think these flowers should go on the piano?"

"That would be lovely," Sarah answered. She had her hands full with the custodian, who was being contrary about leaving his regular work to tend to this function. The models were still arriving, all of them members of the Ladies' Auxiliary, and some of them near panic, now that the time had come to walk out in front of a crowd.

"May I have your attention?" Maggie shouted over the din of raised voices. She moved to the microphone and finally got quiet from the group. "We have too much confusion here. You two," she pointed to two women, "finish putting the flowers on the tables. We'll close the cafeteria in ten minutes and begin charging an admission fee," she directed toward the diners. "Models, follow Dr. Madison down this hall to the room where you will be dressing. The clothes are there and numbered. A corresponding numbered list of models is taped to the wall. Check it and go ahead and change into your first outfit. Is the woman here who's going to narrate?"

Heads turned, looking about. "Fran's not here yet," someone said.

"Who's in charge of refreshments?" Maggie asked. She looked at the woman who raised her hand. "Is everything under control there?"

"We'll be setting things out by one-thirty, so the guests can be served as they walk in."

"All right, fine. Does anyone here not know her job?" Silence. "Good. Let's get things finished up."

Sarah gave her friend the okay sign, thumb and index finger forming a circle, then led the models to the area designated as the dressing room. It was actually the doctors' lounge, and a volunteer had posted a sign that directed the doctors to a conference room for lunch.

The models began changing clothes, and a few minutes later Maggie appeared, looking a little frazzled around the edges, but still in charge. Sarah admired her friend. At times she appeared scatterbrained, but she knew her business.

"Do you all know the route you take around the tables? Remember, pause at each one when you are asked to. We're here to sell these clothes and make money for your hospital."

As soon as she quit speaking, the chatter rose to a fever pitch. Maggie grabbed Sarah and took her over to a corner away from the center of the noise.

"Where's Fran, the narrator?"

"I don't know."

"I told her to be here at one."

"I'll go call her. Is the pianist here?"

"Yes. She's getting set up. Pull that scarf over to the side," Maggie directed one of the models.

"I'm out of here," Sarah said, glad to escape the chaos. She walked briskly toward the nurses' station to use the phone, but ran into Fran before she had gone many steps.

"There you are. Maggie's been asking for you," she said as she ushered the woman toward the dressing room.

"Dr. Madison," Fran whispered. "I've been practicing so much, my voice is gone."

Just what they needed. One more thing to deal with. "Oh. Well, let's find Maggie." Sarah pushed open the door and motioned for Maggie to come out in the hall. "Go on in," she told Fran.

"What?" Maggie barked as she joined Sarah.

"You've heard of hysterical blindness?" Maggie nodded. "Our narrator has a case of hysterical dumbness. She can't talk. My diagnosis, without a thorough exam, is a temporary case of stage fright."

"I knew working with these amateurs was going to be a real pain."

"Calm down, Maggie. You've got a script. It shouldn't be hard to find another reader."

Maggie shot her a sly look. "No, it won't be hard. Come here." She picked up a script and thrust it at Sarah. "You've been to my fashion shows, and you got me into this. Read!"

"Now, Maggie, there's got to be someone else. You read it."

"Can't. I've got to make sure each model is decked out right and enters on cue. There's no other way, Sarah. Those women are basket cases. They'll need me to tell them every step to take."

"Well, surely—"

"No, Sarah, there isn't time. Now take this and go over it so you're familiar with the terms."

"But I was going to sit with Marshall."

"That's too bad. Ellen can baby-sit him." Maggie glanced at her watch. "Twenty-four minutes until curtain. The show must go on and all that stuff."

"All right, all right. But I'll get you for this, Maggie."

Sarah took the script and got a cup of coffee from the volunteer in the cafeteria. The place was beginning to fill, so she took a seat at an empty table by the microphone and skimmed the script. She could do this, but she was getting butterflies thinking of Marshall watching her.

"Sarah." She looked up to see Ellen. "Is this the best table in the house?"

"No. I'm the new narrator. Would you sit with Marshall and Jason?"

"Of course," Ellen said. "I've been waiting to meet those men."

"I've got to go over this." Sarah motioned to the papers in her hand. "When the men come in, I'll introduce you. Be nice to them, and don't tell Marshall I'm a doctor. I'll do that in private after the show. Do you have the check?" After her mental anguish over this dare, she wanted to make sure the end and the reward were in sight.

"Right here," Ellen said and patted her pocket. "Don't worry about the men. I'll take care of them." She found a table near the center of the room. Within ten minutes the men arrived, and Marshall made a beeline for Sarah. She explained the situation, left the men with Ellen, and hurried to the dressing room.

"Five minutes till show time," Maggie was telling the models. "Are you ready?" she asked as soon as she saw Sarah. "Are they here?"

"Yes, on both counts. Ellen is with Marshall and Jason. Are we starting on the dot of two?"

"Unless people are still paying to get in."

It was ten after by the time Sarah stepped in front of the microphone. She looked out on a packed house, said a quick prayer for courage, and took a deep breath. "Good afternoon, ladies and gentlemen." She glanced at Marshall and Jason, two of about ten men in the crowd. "Ambassadors and the Ladies' Auxiliary of Children's Research Hospital present a 'Step into Fall.' Our first model, wearing. . ."

For an hour Sarah read and the models turned and walked and twirled. As the models strutted out for the finale, Sarah glanced at Marshall's table. She had been sneaking looks every chance she had, at risk of losing her place in the script. He did not look bored, but rather was very attentive. She saw him stop one model and ask a question. The pianist kept playing and audience conversations could not be heard. Too bad she could not read lips, for Marshall's table was carrying on quite a low-pitched conversation.

The fashion show was over, and it was not as bad as Marshall had anticipated. Ellen had kept a quiet conversation going. She knew quite a bit about him, and asked about the museum and the ball game.

"Did you talk to Sarah this morning?" Ellen asked.

"No. She spent the night with her parents after we picked them up from the airport."

"You met Sarah's parents?" she asked, her eyes wide.

"Yes, they seem quite nice," Marshall said, although that had not been his first impression of Dr. Madison.

"Hal's never met her parents," Ellen announced.

"Is that right?" Marshall asked, glad to hear that the esteemed Dr. Mosley did not know Sarah nearly as well as he had implied.

"You've met Hal?" Ellen asked.

"Yes. And I don't like him," Marshall said with a smile.

"Me, neither," Ellen agreed. "You and Sarah are much better suited."

"Thanks. I couldn't agree more." Marshall wondered just how much she knew about his relationship with Sarah.

"Are you going to see Sarah after tomorrow?" Ellen asked.

"I hope to." Marshall had had enough of the quiz. "What did you think of the show, Jason?" he asked in an effort to change the subject from himself and Sarah.

"Interesting. Where's Maggie?"

As soon as he asked the question, the models filed into a straight line at the front of the room, and Sarah called Maggie into the cafeteria. A young girl handed Sarah a bouquet of roses, which she presented to Maggie amid applause from the models and the audience.

"Maggie's a nice person," Ellen said as soon as the noise died down.

"Yes, she is," Jason agreed. "And yes, I'm going to see her after I leave. I hope she'll come to Denver for a few days."

"Is it that obvious that I'm trying to find out how things are between you?" Ellen asked. "I don't mean to pry, but I'm interested in their welfare."

"You have nothing to worry about," Marshall said. "They're both in good hands. If you'll excuse us, we need to be getting back to the conference." That was not entirely true. Oh, there was one last workshop going on, but he did not intend to sit in on it. What he needed was to get out of this crowd of women and the inquisition.

Other guests were milling about, admiring the dresses on the models and the ones that were wheeled in on a long rack. Marshall and Jason made their way to where Sarah and Maggie were standing. Although Sarah had offered to give him a tour of the hospital after the show, Marshall was feeling uncomfortable with all these women around. The high-pitched chatter nearly deafened him, and it looked as if Sarah could be tied up for some time.

"Nice job," Marshall said. "We've got to be going, but I'll see you tonight."

"Can't you stay?" she asked, then was immediately besieged by auxiliary women.

"No. I'll take that tour tomorrow before I head to Neosho, so you can enjoy your friends now." He found it hard to stand next to her and not touch her. Yet this was not the place for holding hands or putting his arm around her and pulling her close.

"Marshall, I'll meet you at the hotel," Sarah said.

"Oh, I can pick you up," he said.

"No. I can come with Maggie and you can take me. . ." Her voice trailed off as she turned to acknowledge the woman who had grabbed her arm and in a loud voice congratulated her on a magnificent show.

Marshall took her free hand and squeezed it. "I'll see you at the hotel at six-thirty," he said and turned to leave. He stopped by the table at the exit and talked to the woman taking dress orders and asked that Sarah pick out a dress as a gift from him. He quickly wrote out a check.

"Nice gesture," Jason said as they walked outside.

"It's for the hospital," Marshall said and shrugged. He took a breath of fresh air. "Good to be out of there."

❧

Sarah did not normally resort to violence, but she wanted to smack the loud-mouthed woman who had hold of her arm. Instead she thanked her for coming, then turned to the other well-wishers. "I didn't get to tell him," she said to Maggie.

"You can tell him in privacy in three hours. Be better that way than here."

Maggie could have a point. Telling him at the hospital might be a bit of overkill. Still, she wished she had that moment of telling him she was a doctor behind her.

"Okay, Ellen. The check, please," Sarah said.

Ellen made an elaborate gesture and reached into the pocket of her suit jacket. "Fifty-thousand dollars to the leukemia lab at Children's Research Hospital. This dare was worth every penny of it."

"Good," Sarah said as she stuck the check in her purse. "We'll stretch every penny as far as it will go." And, she thought, it was worth every effort she had made in not revealing her profession to Marshall. "Dr. Madison," one of the volunteers called to her from beside the clothes rack.

Sarah walked over to the area where the guests were going through the clothes. It looked as if quite a few outfits were gone, a good sign for the fund-raiser.

"Dr. Marshall Adams," the volunteer read from the check, "bought you a dress. Which one would you like?"

"Oh," Sarah said. A pleased smile settled on her lips, and she was touched by his thoughtfulness.

"Did I hear right, Sarah? Marshall bought you a dress?" Ellen asked. "I like the red one, and I sure like Marshall. You should snap him up."

"Thanks, I might. The red one's pretty. I'll try it on."

"Try this black one, too," Maggie said. "It'll set off your hair and be perfect for tonight."

"It will, won't it? Be right back."

Sarah modeled the dresses for her friends then glanced at the price tag of the black one. "Oh, this is too expensive."

"He paid more than that," said the volunteer. "The rest was to go to the hospital.

"You'd better grab him, Sarah," Ellen said. "Or I'm going to invite all my single friends over to meet him."

"Don't send out invitations yet," Sarah said with a laugh. "Give me tonight to make an impression on him."

❧

It was after five by the time Sarah made it home. She showered, washed her hair, and was putting the finishing touches on her makeup when the phone rang. "Dr. Madison, this is Nurse Richardson. Dr. Lewis has broken his leg," she said in a matter-of-fact tone. "He's asking for you to come see him immediately."

"Is he all right?" Sarah asked, concern in her voice.

"He will be after it's cast. Right now he demands to talk to you before he lets them knock him out and set it."

"I'll be right there."

She slipped on her new dress and checked the clock. Six. She called the hotel. Marshall did not answer, and the desk clerk came back on the phone and asked if she would like to leave a message.

"This is Sarah Madison. Tell Marshall Adams that I'll be late, but I'll be there. Thanks."

There really was no time to explain. She might try to reach him again from the hospital once she knew how late she would be. She was thankful that she had changed her mind and decided to drive herself to the hotel instead of riding with Maggie. She raced for her car and automatically headed for the hospital.

❧

Marshall saw the flashing light on his phone as soon as he walked into the bedroom from the bathroom. He had shut the door or he might have heard the ring over the shower.

The desk clerk informed him that Sarah would be late. But there was no explanation. What had happened? If she had been hurt, surely she would have said so. He hung up the phone, then picked it up and punched in Sarah's number. It rang eleven times before he hung it up again.

He pulled his navy blue, three-piece suit from the closet. No way was Hal Mosley going to show him up tonight. The intellectual side of his brain told him that Hal was no threat to his relationship with Sarah. However, his emotional side was afraid of Hal. Afraid of his reputation and his long friendship with Sarah.

He was tying his tie for the second time when Ed knocked on his door.

"Come on in," he invited after Ed had already entered the room. Marshall buttoned his vest and slipped on his suit jacket. "Sarah's going to be late. Come on, we'll wait in the lobby." For once he did not mind his friend's companionship. Talking with him would make the time go faster while he waited for Sarah.

The elevator took the men down to the lobby. Ed and Marshall got off as Maggie got on.

"Sarah's going to be a little late," Marshall told Maggie before the elevator door closed. "Save a place for us if you and Jason go in first."

❧

When the hotel desk came back on the line again, Sarah asked for Jason's room. Maybe Marshall was there. But he wasn't.

"Please tell him to go on into the banquet. I'll be there. And, Jason, tell him to trust me. There's been an emergency, and I'll explain everything when I see him. I know it will confuse him, but I can explain." Sarah felt as if she were babbling. She did not want to tell Jason about the dare, but she was worried about Marshall's reaction once he learned she was a doctor. And he would learn it shortly, and not in the manner she had planned.

"I've got that, Sarah. I'll see that he gets the word. See you later," Jason rang off.

Sarah replaced the receiver and smiled across the small room at Dr. Lewis, who lay on a hospital bed. He was pale, and she could tell he was in pain.

"My notes are here, Sarah. You won't have any trouble reading them. I had Lorraine type them up."

"I'm sure I can read them just fine," Sarah said and smiled reassuringly at her boss. "Why don't I call the bone setter in and get you all fixed up?"

"Don't try that patient talk on me, Sarah. I know your style. They're going to hurt me, and you know it. Just think, I'll be the oldest patient at Children's Research."

"If you don't behave and let them get to work, I'll have you transferred to Mercy. And you won't get all the special pampering you've been receiving from our nurses." She said it with a laugh, but shook a finger at him. He needed that leg set now.

"Now, Sarah. Just give the speech one time so I can answer any questions you might have. Then I'll let the quacks at me. I was so honored to be chosen for the closing address," he mumbled. "And this had to happen. I'm such a klutz."

On his way to the hotel, he had stopped by the lab to check an experiment, had spilled some water, and then slipped in it.

Sarah read the speech out loud, stopping several times for Dr. Lewis to clarify points. It was after seven when they finished.

"How about one more time, Sarah?"

"No. You promised you'd let them work on your leg, and you're going to. I'll read it again before I go on stage. I'll do the best I can."

"Oh, I'm not worried about that. You'll do a better job than I would."

"Thanks for the vote of confidence. I need it." Sarah pushed the button for the nurse to come in. "What time were you scheduled to go on?"

"After eight."

A nurse walked in, followed closely by two more nurses. "About time," she grumbled. "We've been ready for an hour."

"Take care," Sarah said and patted the doctor on the hand. "I'll check back in with you after the speech. Oh, and Dr. Lewis, I have something to show you." She smiled apologetically at the nurses for the delay and dug in her purse. She handed Ellen's check to her boss.

"I don't know how much we made on the fashion show for the hospital, but this check is just for our lab."

"Why did Kent Crawford give us this money?" he asked.

"Actually it's his wife, Ellen, who's behind it. It's a long story, and I'll tell you after your leg is set."

He handed the check back to her. "All right then, let's go," he directed the nurses. "Have that story ready," he said to Sarah before he was wheeled out into the hall.

"Good luck," she called after him. Sarah gathered up her notes. She felt sure that Dr. Lewis would be fine; she had seen the X ray as soon as she had walked into the hospital. Because of his age, it would take some time to heal, but it was a clean break. He had had some medicine for pain before she saw him, but until after he saw Sarah, he had refused the medicine that would make him drowsy. He was tough. She admired that streak in him. She admired everything about him, but he had surely put her in an awkward situation.

❧

On the way to the hotel, Sarah tried to go over the speech, but without the notes in front of her, her mind refused to think along those lines and instead focused on Marshall. What would his reaction be when he saw her on stage? Maybe she could pull Marshall out of the banquet so she could talk with him before she gave her speech. She certainly could not tell him in front of a table of people; she discarded that idea. There was no time; she needed to go over that speech again. At ten minutes before eight, she arrived at the hotel. The master of ceremonies had been informed that she would be replacing Dr. Lewis, and a hotel employee had been dispatched to tell him Sarah had arrived. Sarah paced the hall, waiting for the doctor to come out of the banquet room.

"Would you like to come to the head table?" he asked when he appeared. "There isn't time for you to eat, but we can arrange for something afterward."

Something to eat was the least of Sarah's worries. She was soon to face a mob of doctors who had been practicing medicine many more years than she. And Marshall was in there, too. "I'd like to reread this speech before I go in," Sarah said.

"Fine. When I introduce you, enter from the side door, which is right beside the head table." He took her down another hall and showed her the door.

"I'll send someone out right before we're ready for you."

With that he slipped back inside the banquet hall.

There was no chair around, and Sarah did not dare go

hunt for a place to sit. A dim light fixture provided her only light. Obviously the hall was used for employees and not guests of the hotel. Sarah stood under the light and studied Dr. Lewis's notes, talking aloud in a quiet tone.

All too soon a man of about fifty came out into the hall. "We're ready for you." He kept the door open a crack, and Sarah heard the master of ceremonies tell a joke and the audience respond appreciatively. She hoped they would be as receptive to her. She strained to hear her introduction.

"Our closing speaker was to have been Dr. Warner Lewis, noted research scientist from Children's Research Hospital right here in Kansas City. Due to an accident, Dr. Lewis is at this moment having his broken leg set. In his place he sent his assistant. He assured me that she knows every bit as much as he does and is prettier, besides. Please welcome Dr. Sarah Madison."

eleven

Marshall stared at the stage in shock as Sarah walked out, looking as calm as if she gave speeches every day of her life, which as far as he knew, she just might. He knew his mouth was hanging open, but he could not take it all in. So this was the meaning of her cryptic message to Jason. She would explain everything later. She was a doctor, not a high school health teacher. Why had she lied? Maggie reached over the empty seat that separated them and patted his hand. "She'll explain everything, Marshall. She wanted to tell you, but we wouldn't let her."

"You wouldn't let her?"

"Well," she hesitated. "She'll tell you when she's finished. Let's listen."

Marshall nodded and sat very still, but he did not hear a word of Sarah's address. He watched her every move, her every gesture, but did not listen to what she said. His head was spinning. He had trusted her. Both Jason and Ed had laughed at his blind trust, and he had been blind, all right.

She was wearing one of the dresses he had seen at the fashion show. The one she had probably bought with his check. He felt used. He felt foolish. But most of all he felt betrayed. Tonight was the night he was prepared to declare his love. And what was she thinking? That tonight was the night she would laugh at Dr. Marshall Adams? The twenty-five-minute speech lasted half a lifetime. As soon as it was over, Marshall scooted into the empty chair by Maggie's and demanded the story.

"I can't tell you," she whispered. "But she really likes you, Marshall. Don't be mad at her."

"Don't be mad at her? She lied to me. I trusted her and she lied to me. And you say don't be mad? She said she taught health."

"She teaches interns. She said she wouldn't lie to you; she would just avoid the truth." Maggie bit her lip as if she had said too much. She turned away as the master of ceremonies introduced the conference chairman.

Marshall looked around at the people at his table. From their expressions, Jason and Ed had not known that Sarah was a doctor. But the thorn in his side, Dr. Hal Mosley, was sitting across from him and leaned forward to make a comment.

"Sarah's very good, don't you think?" Hal said proudly. "She's an excellent doctor, but she gets too involved sometimes."

That was the last straw. The pompous Dr. Harold Mosley had known about Sarah's little joke all along. What an idiot Marshall was. Dr. Mosley had sat at breakfast with him only two days ago, making ownership statements about Dr. Sarah Madison, and now he knew they were true. Mosley had never once let on that Sarah was a doctor. If he hadn't been in on the joke, he would surely have said something that would have told Marshall that Sarah was a doctor. And tonight Hal purposely sat at their table so that he could watch Marshall's reaction.

Marshall stared at Sarah. She was seated beside the new president of the AMA and had her head inclined his way to hear what he was saying. But her eyes were searching the audience. For him? Probably. She wanted to see the effect of her little joke on him. He knew she could not see him. His table was at the back of the room and the house lights had been turned off with only lights on the dais to spotlight the head table.

❧

Sarah peered through the darkness that engulfed the audience. She could make out only the shapes of tables and bodies. The lights shining down on her were too bright for her to see through the dimness that hid Marshall.

What must he be thinking? She tried tactfully to hush the man beside her, for he was making small talk, and she thought he could at least give the chairman of the conference the courtesy of listening.

The traditional thank-yous that ended the convention took forever. Finally it was over, and Sarah stood as soon as the lights in the banquet room were turned back on. The men at the head table grouped around her and shook her hand, congratulating her on a fine job on such short notice. She brushed their praise aside and stepped off the dais, making a beeline for Maggie. Her friend's red hair had been a beacon and she homed in on it. Marshall stood with his back to her. She came up behind him and took his arm, leading him a few steps away from the others.

"Marshall, I can explain," she said.

"Please do," he said coldly, his arms folded across his chest.

He was furious and she did not blame him. This was not the way he was supposed to find out. She took a deep breath and began.

"I took a dare at that restaurant Monday night that I could get you to the fashion show this afternoon. My friends said I'm usually too serious, so I promised not to tell you I was a doctor, so I wouldn't intimidate you and scare you off. We didn't know you were a doctor, too. I got you to the show. I wanted to tell you several times. I'm sorry, but it was important. You see—"

"Sarah, you did a magnificent job," Hal said as he came up beside her and gave her a congratulatory hug. "How's Warner doing?"

"He'll be all right. It was a clean break," Sarah answered and pulled away from him.

Marshall positively glowered.

"Marshall didn't tell us you were a doctor," said the chunky fellow who was with Marshall that first night in the restaurant. He stood behind Marshall. Jason and Maggie joined him.

"Well, I am," Sarah said.

"Marshall didn't know," Jason explained. "There was some sort of dare that Sarah could get him to go to a fashion show."

Sarah glanced at Maggie, who shrugged. Obviously, she hadfilled Jason in on the bet.

"And did you?" the fellow asked.

"Yes," Sarah said, watching Marshall's explosive expression.

"You took a dare about him and he took a dare about you." The fellow laughed. Sarah stared at him.

"That's enough, Ed," Marshall cut in.

"No, it isn't. What dare?" Sarah demanded.

Ed looked from one to the other and shrugged. "Ah, you acted like a glacier in that restaurant. We dared him to melt the iceberg and get you to go out with him. Prove that the Adams charm was still strong.

Sarah felt as if she had been hit in the stomach. She turned her head and closed her eyes. So this whole week had been a charade.

Hal stepped in for her. "Of all the sophomoric pranks! Come on, Sarah, I'll take you home."

Sarah did not answer, but turned and walked out of the banquet hall with Hal following. She crossed the lobby and strode out the door to the parking garage.

"Sarah," Hal called to her from the door. "Wait, Sarah!"

She did not want to talk to anyone and certainly not to Hal. But by the time she had her key out of her purse and had unlocked the car door, he was at her side.

"Sarah, let me drive you." He put his arm solicitously on her shoulder.

"Leave me alone, Hal," she said and moved away from his touch.

"I know you're upset about that silly dare. And I don't blame you. The man's obviously a cad. I never did like him."

"You don't know anything about it, Hal. So just keep quiet."

"Well, at least nothing happened between you two that you would regret later. He may be a smooth operator, but you shot him down."

"Shut up, Hal." She pulled the door open and sat down but Hal held the door. "Get out of my way. I mean it. Stay out of my life now, and stay out of it later!"

He turned loose of the door and she slammed it. "You don't know what you're saying, Sarah." She could hear his loud voice through the closed window.

"Oh yes, I do." With Hal standing inches from the car, Sarah surged out of the parking space. As she moved forward, she had the grace to look in her rearview mirror to make sure she had not run over his foot. Not that she cared. She had told him to get out of the way. She drove home in record time, pulled into her garage, and rested her head on the steering wheel. She was weary. The stress of giving the speech and the fear of Marshall's reaction to her deception had drained her. Still, she was angry and hurt that he had asked her out on a dare. Was that his sole purpose in pursuing her and why he was so persistent? That was why he had introduced himself to her that first night at the restaurant. She had thanked God that he had approached her instead of her having to ask him out. Now she understood why.

Sarah lifted her head from the wheel. She was tired. She had not slept well at her parents' house and she needed some sleep. Then she would sort through all that had transpired in the last hour.

How fast her future had disintegrated. She pushed the remote control button to close the garage door and climbed out of the car. The house seemed empty as she dragged herself through the kitchen door and found the strength to put on the kettle for a cup of soothing tea. She had had no dinner, but the thought of food turned her stomach.

Two nights ago in this very kitchen, Marshall had fixed her soup and toasted bread. He had been so kind, so understanding. Was that an act? The kettle whistled and Sarah mechanically made a cup of tea. She carried it into the living room and collapsed on the couch, her mind whirling. Something did not add up. If they had merely dared him to get her to go out with him, he had accomplished that on Monday night.

Before she lost her courage, she dialed the hotel. There was unfinished business between them, and she wanted it settled.

"Marshall Adams's room, please," she said to the desk clerk.

"I'm sorry. Dr. Adams checked out a few minutes ago."

So this was it. She would never see him again. They had deceived each other with dares, lies, and manipulation.

The love that she had felt withered inside her.

"Thank you," she finally mustered, and hung up the phone.

So he was gone. And why would he leave, if he had nothing to hide himself? If only Dr. Lewis had not broken his leg.

Her sense of responsibility took over, and she reached for the phone and dialed the hospital.

"How's your most famous patient?" she asked the head nurse.

"Dr. Lewis is a real grouch. He wouldn't take general anesthetic. Gave him a local. He told me to put you through as soon as you called."

Sarah talked to her boss for a few minutes. His voice was groggy, and he spoke slowly. As soon as she assured him the speech was well-received, she felt he would quit fighting the medicine and go to sleep.

Ten minutes later, from her bedroom phone, Sarah called the nurse back and found that Dr. Lewis was sleeping. She unzipped her new dress that Marshall had bought for her. He had surely paid a premium price for the time they had spent together. That thought made her feel bought, and she hung the dress out of sight at the back of her closet.

She had been bought. She had allowed Ellen to buy her honesty for fifty-thousand dollars. Every person has his price, didn't the old saying go? Who would have thought she was worth only fifty-thousand dollars? She was so confused. One minute she was furious with Marshall, and the next she was missing him and wondering how he was feeling and where he was.

Maybe he would come to his senses and call her. Of course, that's what he would do. He was not the type to run from a confrontation. Actually, she was the one who had fled the banquet hall. He would give her time to cool off, then he would phone. After donning her nightgown, she lay down on the bed to await his call.

She stared at the ceiling for the longest time, watching the patterns that car lights made as they drove by on the street below. After a while the lights became more infrequent.

"Dear God," she prayed, "I've really messed things up. What do I do now? What do I do?"

When the phone rang at midnight, she was still awake. It had to be Marshall. He had gotten over his initial anger and wanted to talk.

It was Maggie. "Are you all right, Sarah?"

"No, I'm not all right, but I'll survive."

"I've told Jason everything, all about my dare, too. And you know what? He loves me anyway. He's asked me to go to Denver next weekend, and I'm going. We'll see each other as often as we can and get to know each other. We want to be sure that this relationship is right for both of us."

"That's wonderful, Maggie," Sarah said and meant it. At least one of them had come out ahead on this dare. "I'm happy for both of you."

"Sarah, about Marshall. I told him you wanted to tell him about being a doctor, but we wouldn't let you. I tried to smooth it over, but he was angry."

"What exactly did he say?" Sarah asked. She could barely breathe, and her heart was beating double time.

"He said he'd trusted you, but you lied to him. That's about all."

"I see. Well, that's that." Sarah tried to sound as if it did not matter. It was not Maggie's fault that she had let herself be talked into the dare. She had thought it would be an experiment to see if all men were like Jeff and felt threatened by an intelligent woman. Well, she had her answer, or did she? She was too confused to even think about that angle.

"Sarah, about Marshall's dare. He'd been talking about how women were after him because of prestige and money. Then you showed up, and they thought you looked glacial, and Jason and Ed dared him to see if the Adams charm was still there without a woman knowing he was a doctor. It's really no big thing. He told you he was a doctor as soon as you agreed to a cup of coffee with him. Now he's upset because he thinks you lied to him."

Sarah stifled a sob.

"Call him, Sarah," Maggie urged. "Just a minute." Sarah heard mumbled voices in the background. "Jason said Marshall cares about you. He's just upset and hurt."

"I see."

"Sarah, if you want me to come over—"

"No," Sarah cut her off. "I'm fine. I'll probably call him and get this worked out. 'Bye."

She hung up an instant before tears poured down her cheeks again. She was in the right, and he was in the wrong. Or was it the other way around? Her mind spun and the tears continued to fall.

twelve

Marshall turned into the driveway of the Valley. As he followed the winding lane to the house and parked his car in the detached garage, the clock on the dashboard read 1:03. He had run into such hard rain, he had had to pull over to the side of the road and wait for the thunderstorm to move on.

As exhausted as he was, he was still furious with Sarah. During the long drive home, he had replayed the entire week in his mind. She was some actress.

His house had that musty, closed-up smell. He walked around opening windows, then fixed a cup of coffee and sat in the huge, brown, overstuffed chair that faced the fireplace.

He felt empty inside, and his thoughts were racing a mile a minute back to Kansas City.

The whole week had been phony. He reexamined their initial meeting. At the time, he had been amazed at how quickly Sarah had agreed to have coffee with him. Now he understood. What would her approach have been if he had not taken the initiative? The conversation about intelligent women played in his mind. Maybe there was a bit of honesty in her. At least she did not follow through on that routine. Astrological signs! Hah! The ball game, the museum. Were Sarah's brother and sister-in-law in on the big joke? And what about her father? Had Marshall actually told the man that he was planning on marrying his daughter? She was an excellent actress, he thought again. He had trusted her. She had said she taught high school health. No, she had said she taught health, but never said where. He had assumed it was in a high school, but he had never asked her. If it had not been for Hal Mosley, he might think there had been some horrible mistake. She had wanted to meet him before the banquet. Maybe she was going to tell him then. Maggie had said she wanted to tell him, but the dare would not let her. She had not planned on giving that closing address. Dr. Lewis' breaking his leg was an accident. But what if she had not planned on telling him at all? Why did she take the dare? She did not seem like the type of woman who went around taking crazy dares.

The late hour and the strain of the trip home were undermining his desire to stay awake and sort through his relationship with Sarah one more time.

Did he love Sarah? Yes. Although all evidence pointed otherwise, he could not bring himself to believe that Sarah was capable of leading him on so callously.

He shook his head to clear it. His heart was overruling his head, and he had to make order of it. He should never have left Kansas City without talking to her, hearing her side of the whole affair. He kept coming back to Hal Mosley. Marshall thought of himself as a fair man, but he hoped Mosley would drop off the face of the earth. And he really did not know the man. He set his cup down on the table next to the chair, closed his eyes, and took a deep breath. He should have followed her home instead of coming back to Neosho.

So, she was a doctor instead of a health teacher. Big deal. Maybe she had a good reason for taking the dare. Maybe she needed to be known for herself instead of her profession. He had felt that way before, wanted people to think of him as a man instead of a doctor. He thought about the women who were so impressed with his credentials.

He sat up straight. He had forgotten about his dare. She had stormed out before he could explain it was not a big deal, and he had been too angry to stop her. It had started as a fun event, just as Sarah's dare had that night in the restaurant. But she did not know that. What must she be thinking about him? He was a fool, and it was none of Sarah's doing. He had felt inferior to Mosley. A general practitioner could not compete with a heart surgeon. But Sarah did not care about his profession. Hadn't Maggie said that Sarah did not even know he was a doctor when she had accepted her dare? He had to talk to her. Should he call her? No, he needed to see her reaction as they talked. He would go back to Kansas City. Yes, that was what he would do.

Several hours later, the sun streaming through the open window woke him. He stretched to ease the cramped muscles that came from sleeping in a chair.

It was after nine. He felt better after his sleep, and his first thought was that he would return to Kansas City as soon as he had seen his patients. He walked outside on the porch. It was cool this morning, a definite nip in the air. It was always cooler in the Valley than it was in town. He looked across at the giant steps on the terraced hills. He loved this place. It gave him a sense of well-being. Everything would work out, one way or another, and he felt hope again. If Sarah rejected him, he would be hurt, but at least it would be out in the open and settled without this awful unfinished feeling. And he could come to grips with it. But if they worked things out, if they could find a way to merge their complex lives. . . . He smiled. She would find a sense of place here, too.

❧

Sarah carried a cup of coffee into Dr. Lewis's room. He

was propped up in bed for breakfast with his newly cast leg lying outside the covers to dry.

She had awakened by six, and although she was still tired, she opted for action instead of analyzing things gone wrong. Dr. Lewis would need her. And she needed to check on Joey.

"Sarah, you work too much," Dr. Lewis told her. "You should be out having fun instead of baby-sitting an old man with a broken leg."

Sarah took a big gulp of coffee. She was getting the same song, second verse, from her boss as she had had from the Fab Five.

"I probably need more balance in my life," she said. "And I'm working on that."

"Good. I've been worried about you. Have you ever thought about getting out of clinical research and setting up your own practice?"

He had read her mind. In the night she had examined not only her failed relationship with Marshall, but her life's goals and expectations, too. Even when Marshall thought she volunteered time at the hospital, he had suggested she find another place to give her time, such as a hospital where children got well instead of died. A person could take only so much pressure, and she had had her limit.

"I've given it some thought lately," she said. "But I don't want to give up on the children."

"You wouldn't be. You'd be helping in another way. We don't know what causes leukemia, but keeping children healthy and discovering the disease early if it struck could give children a happy ending. Now, tell me the story behind the check you showed me last night."

Sarah finished relating the tale in a dispassionate voice then left for early church. She thought more about opening her own practice as she drove to her church.

As she studied the smiling faces in the children's choir, she imagined what it would be like to see children on a regular basis for healthy checkups instead of saying a final good-bye to them as she had Andrea.

She returned to the hospital a little after nine as she had promised Dr. Lewis she would check on him again. Besides, what else could she do with her Sunday? She did not want to be alone and let her mind focus on Marshall.

"Dr. Madison, you've had a message." A nurse stopped her at the main desk and handed her a phone slip.

Could it be that Marshall called at last? She was disappointed to read her parents' number on the message. With a heavy heart, she called home.

"Sarah, I knew you'd show up at the hospital," her mother said.

"Dr. Lewis has a broken leg and is our oldest patient now," she explained.

"Yes, I heard. A friend of your dad's called after your speech last night. He said you were fabulous. We're so proud. Are you working today?"

"No. Just checking on things."

"Good. If you and Marshall have no other plans, we were hoping you'd come out for Sunday dinner."

"Thanks, Mom, but Marshall has already gone back to Neosho."

"Oh, that's too bad. I was hoping to get to know him better. Well, next time he's up you could bring him out."

"There won't be a next time," Sarah admitted. She did not want to explain everything, but she did not want her mother harboring any false assumptions.

"What's wrong, Sarah?"

"We had a disagreement." That really simplified what had

happened, but she could not tell her mother about the dare.

"Don't worry, dear. He'll be back. He's already told your dad that he plans to marry you if you'll have him."

"What?" Sarah could not believe what she heard. "What did you say?"

"Oops. I guess Marshall didn't get around to asking you before this little disagreement."

"He told Dad he wants to marry me?" Sarah had to have it exactly.

"Yes. That's what they were discussing in the kitchen Friday night. So, don't be too upset about your little spat, Sarah. It'll all work out, if you love him." Sarah could hear the question in her mother's voice.

"Yes, I do," Sarah said softly, and began unwinding the telephone cord she had twisted into a knot. "I know this seems sudden to you—"

"Not at all," her mother interrupted. "I knew I wanted to marry your father the night I met him. Some things are just meant to be. And I think you and Marshall make a strong couple."

"Yes, we do," Sarah agreed. "Thanks for the dinner invitation, but I think I'll decline. I need to talk to Marshall."

"Good idea, dear. Good luck."

"Thanks, Mom." Sarah hung up the receiver with a lighter heart. Surely Marshall would not have told her father he intended to marry her if he did not mean it.

With new hope, she fairly skipped to Dr. Lewis's room.

"Is there anything I can get for you, Doctor?" she asked.

"No, Sarah. Will you be back today?"

"Probably not. I'll be out of town most of the day." It all depended on Marshall. She could not discuss everything with him on the phone. She needed to see his eyes, read his expressions.

"Take care, Sarah. He'd better treat you right."

"What?"

"You came in here earlier like a whipped pup. Now your eyes are sparkling again. One plus one equals a man in your life and my guess is he's the one who attended the fashion show."

Sarah laughed. "You missed your calling. You should have been a detective." She sobered a bit. "I'll let you know how it works out." With a smile and a wave, she left the room and strode down the hospital corridor, and the minute she stepped outside, she ran for her car.

Pulling out a Missouri map from the glove compartment, she studied it a moment. Four lane highway most of the way. Her gas gauge registered full. She drove the most expedient route out of town and within minutes was on the highway heading south. She checked her watch. Nine-thirty exactly.

❧

Marshall walked around the house and checked to see that no damage had been done to his house from wind or rain while he had been gone. Everything looked the same. The hills beckoned to him. He wanted to climb them, but time marched on.

It was ten-thirty before he had unpacked his luggage from the convention, showered, and driven to the hospital. His patients were all doing well. Even the elderly man with pneumonia was much better. Marshall read his latest X rays and agreed with Dr. Pierce's diagnosis. Only a slight shadow darkened one corner of one lung. The pneumonia was almost gone. Relieved that his patients were doing well, he now could turn his thoughts toward Sarah and get things straightened out with her.

He strode purposefully out of the hospital and headed

his car for the open road.

❧

Sarah had no idea where the Valley was. Marshall had said it was west of town. Finding the town was easy. Criss-crossing the country roads on the west side was making her more and more nervous about the coming confrontation with Marshall.

She did not know how she would start the conversation and hoped he would help her out. She would be honest and answer any questions he had about the dare. And she had a few questions of her own to ask, too.

She had not passed a farmhouse in the last quarter-mile and was ready to turn back and try another road when she saw the terraced hills ahead. He was right they did look like stairs for giants. A stone arch announced the entrance; right beside it stood a rural mailbox that read: ADAMS, ROUTE 3, BOX 14A.

She had found it! She followed the drive at least an eighth of a mile till she saw the house nestled in the Valley. It belonged there. The A-frame fit in with the terraced hills and tall trees that surrounded it.

She saw no movement anywhere. After parking her car in the graveled area beside a detached garage, she walked to the front porch, which held two rocking chairs at one end and a porch swing at the other. She stood in front of the door, took a deep breath, and rang the bell. No answer. She punched the doorbell again and waited.

He was not home. Where could he be? At the hospital? She walked dejectedly back toward her car, then veered to the garage. There were no windows in the garage door, but two high ones on the side. The window at the rear of the garage revealed a workshop, complete with table saw. Other woodworking tools sat neatly on shelves that lined the one wall she could see.

She did not know that Marshall liked to work with wood. It did not surprise her, though, that he would make things with his hands. But it did point out that there were many things she did not know about him.

The second window was just as revealing. The space for his car was empty. She had hoped he was walking around the hills, as he had told her he liked to do. Now what? Should she wait and hope he would return soon? Should she go to the hospital and try to catch him there? What if he never came home at all? She glanced at her watch. Twelve-thirty. Her stomach told her it was much later, since she had not eaten since a quick lunch the day before. She was finally hungry. No, she was ravenous.

For absolutely no reason, except frustration, she marched to the porch and rang the doorbell again. Reaching for the doorknob, she gave it a quick twist and was amazed when the door opened.

"Marshall?" she called before she stepped inside. She knew he was not there, but she called his name again anyway.

Feeling a little like Goldilocks, she looked around guiltily before she entered, searching for clues to Marshall's personality.

The living room looked neat, but unbalanced. A stone fireplace dominated the room and provided the focus for the conversation area. Instead of the couch facing the fireplace with chairs on each side, the couch was on the side with a big, brown, stuffed chair facing the fireplace. This must be his favorite chair. The ottoman was scooted out a ways from the chair, as if he had gotten up suddenly without pushing it back in place.

She moved quietly to the chair and sat down where he

had been, how many hours ago? She knew he had been here the night before. The windows were opened, and the house had the faint smell of coffee. Climbing out of the deep chair, she walked to the kitchen. On the stove sat a skillet and spatula. Inside the dishwasher were dirty dishes from his breakfast. The refrigerator held the usual assortment of condiments, but lacked the perishables: milk, bacon, and so on. He had not gone shopping since he had been back. Maybe he was doing that now.

The stairs led to a loft with two bedrooms. One room served as a study. The other was his bedroom with the bed neatly made. The bathroom yielded more information. A towel, hanging next to the shower, was still damp from recent use.

The pieces of the puzzle were fitting together for Sarah, who thought Dr. Lewis was not the only one who could have been a detective. Marshall had come home and sat in the brown chair. He had taken a shower and had coffee and fixed something to eat in the skillet for breakfast. Probably an egg.

Eggs sounded pretty good to her right now. Not hesitating more than a moment, she descended the stairs to the kitchen.

❧

Marshall stopped at the traffic light and turned right instead of going straight on the road that led to the highway. What had he read on his flip-a-day calendar that very morning while he was eating breakfast? "Sunday clears away the rust of the whole week." If ever he needed the rust cleared, today was the day. The digital clock on the dashboard told him it was past eleven. Church would have already started, but he turned back anyway and pulled into the parking lot five minutes later. He found a seat in the back pew and listened to the triumphant singing of the choir.

No soft hymns today, but loud alleluias and amens made the windows rattle. He felt his spirits being lifted with the music. When the last strong chords faded, the minister addressed the congregation. The sermon droned on and on, going well past the noon hour, but Marshall did not know what the minister had said. His heart and mind were talking to God about Sarah.

When the service ended, he felt more at peace. And he knew he needed to talk with the woman he loved. But he needed to tackle this in a systematic way. Instead of traipsing all over Kansas City looking for her, he would call first and tell her he was coming. This time when he reached the stop light, he turned toward home to call her. If she was not at her house or at the hospital or at her parents' home, he would head north anyway and have Maggie help him find Sarah. His arched entrance came into sight, and he felt a great relief. Why? He could not explain his feeling. He drove down the lane to his house, and as soon as he saw her car, he knew. God had answered his prayer to work things out with her. She was here, and he also knew everything would be wonderful between them. She would not have driven down here to gloat about the dare.

The front door stood open; he must have left the door unlocked, which he sometimes did. He did not worry about prowlers in the country. She must be inside, but he thought she would come out when he pulled up. He turned off the engine and heard music pouring from the open windows and door.

He smiled to himself. She was making herself right at home. Good. She might like it well enough to want to live here.

His shoes made a sharp tapping sound on the wooden planks of the porch, but still Sarah did not appear. He walked through the open doorway and into the entry. At first he did not see her, then he caught movement in the kitchen. He walked quietly toward her and stood beside the bar and waited.

Sarah had her back to him and was stirring something on the stove. Scrambled eggs. He could smell them now.

Suddenly, she stiffened. She had felt his presence. A whispered, "Marshall," escaped her lips as she turned around.

For a long moment they stared at each other across the room. "Sarah—"

"Marshall, we need to talk."

"Yes, we do," he agreed. "But first I suggest you take care of the eggs."

"Oh, no." The acrid smell of burning eggs reached her nose the second he mentioned them. She turned back to the stove, but it was too late. The eggs were scorched on the bottom and still raw on top. "Too late," she said as she carried the smoking skillet to the sink and deposited the mess in the garbage disposal.

"Too late for the eggs, but not too late for us." Marshall took her by the hand and led her to the living room. "I stopped to call you before I headed back to Kansas City. I wanted to talk to you in person."

She smiled as he motioned for her to sit in the big brown chair. He scooted the ottoman farther out and sat down facing her.

"Now," he said. "Let's hear about the dare."

"I can explain it all, but I'd like to hear about your dare, too."

He grimaced. "I figured you would. I guess we both

have some explaining to do."

Sarah talked first and told him how many times she had started to tell him the truth about being a doctor. "When I took you to the hospital to see Andrea, I thought you'd find out without me telling you. I'm still amazed that no one called me Doctor."

"Why did you take the dare?" Marshall asked.

"I earned fifty-thousand dollars for leukemia research."

"Wow! I had no idea there was incentive like that. I'd have taken the dare myself." He reached for her hand and held it. "I thought it was a joke on me. After much thought, I knew there had to be more to it. That's why I was headed back to see you." He wanted to know one more thing and was apprehensive about bringing it up. If this were going to be an honest relationship, he had to be up front about anything that bothered him. He plunged ahead.

"What about Hal Mosley?"

"What about Hal?"

"Did he know about the dare? He hinted that you two were. . .more than friends."

"Why that jerk!" Sarah was indignant. "You pegged him right the night I introduced you. I've always known he's wanted more in our relationship than I was willing to give. He's a friend, although pompous at times, and he treats me in a condescending manner sometimes. But he knew nothing about the dare. I'm surprised he didn't give me away. Trust me, there's never been a relationship other than friendship between us."

Marshall sighed his relief. "That's what this whole misunderstanding is all about, isn't it? Trust. I'm sorry I didn't follow you home so we could explain everything in Kansas City instead of rushing back here like a hurt fool."

"You aren't a fool, but I know you were hurt."

"Devastated. I couldn't put the whole picture together. I knew you'd lied to me, and I thought the whole week was phony, yet I couldn't believe you were like that. The Sarah I know and love is warm, caring, sensitive, and has a wonderful sense of humor."

"A sense of humor? Really?" At his nod, she continued. "That's what started this whole bet. The Fab Five think I'm too serious and should let loose more. Now, let's hear about your dare," she said.

He stood up and crossed to the fireplace. "It started as a dare. I was attracted to you immediately, and the thought of spending time with you was more than appealing."

"By the way, there was a third dare."

His eyebrows shot up in question.

"We dared Maggie to get Jason to the fashion show without asking him. She used my dare to help her out. Sounds really juvenile, I know. She told Jason all about it."

"How did he take it?"

"The airlines are going to make a fortune on Denver-to-Kansas City airfares. They're going to take turns visiting each other while they get to know each other better. They've both had bad experiences, and they want to be sure before they make a permanent commitment."

"What about you?"

"Me?"

"Do you want more time to make sure, or will you marry me now?"

Sarah closed her eyes and leaned back in the chair. "There are lots of things I don't know about you, but I'm quite sure I want to spend the rest of my life finding out what they are."

"When, Sarah?" He took her hands in his and pulled her

out of the chair and into his arms. They hugged each other, then Sarah lifted her face to receive his kiss.

The kiss was all she had hoped it would be. Anger was missing, but passion and love were in full force when his lips met hers. When he lifted his head, she withdrew slowly.

"Just name the day," he said.

"A month from now." That would give her mother time to arrange a small wedding and let her give notice at the hospital. "We have a few problems to work out."

"Problems?"

"Not major. Just logistics. I have a job in Kansas City, and you have a practice here."

"I'd like to keep my practice, but I could start over if necessary."

"I've been thinking about working in another hospital away from terminally ill children. I've reached my limit. When one of them dies, a little of me dies, too. For now I need to help children get well. Is there a pediatrician in Neosho?"

"You know," he said with a grin, "we don't have a children's specialist here."

"Good."

He kissed her again. When he finished the kiss, she pulled away and grinned up at him.

"Right now I'm so hungry I can hardly think. I haven't eaten since yesterday."

"Come to the kitchen, and I'll rustle something up. Then I'll show you around the Valley and the hills, starting with a tour of your soon-to-be new home. I think you'll love it here."

"Yes, I daresay I will."

A Letter To Our Readers

Dear Reader:

In order that we might better contribute to your reading enjoyment, we would appreciate your taking a few minutes to respond to the following questions. When completed, please return to the following:

Rebecca Germany, Managing Editor
Heartsong Presents
P.O. Box 719
Uhrichsville, Ohio 44683

1. Did you enjoy reading *A Question of Balance*?
   - ❑ Very much. I would like to see more books by this author!
   - ❑ Moderately
     I would have enjoyed it more if ________________

   ____

2. Are you a member of **Heartsong Presents**? ❑Yes ❑No
   If no, where did you purchase this book? ________________

   ____

3. What influenced your decision to purchase this book? (Check those that apply.)

❑ Cover	❑ Back cover copy
❑ Title	❑ Friends
❑ Publicity	❑ Other________________

4. How would you rate, on a scale from 1 (poor) to 5 (superior), the cover design? ________________

5. On a scale from 1 (poor) to 10 (superior), please rate the following elements.

    ___Heroine ___Plot

    ___Hero ___Inspirational theme

    ___Setting ___Secondary characters

6. What settings would you like to see covered in **Heartsong Presents** books?______________________

    ____

    ____

7. What are some inspirational themes you would like to see treated in future books?______________________

    ____

    ____

8. Would you be interested in reading other **Heartsong Presents** titles? ❑ Yes ❑ No

9. Please check your age range:
    ❑ Under 18 ❑ 18-24 ❑ 25-34
    ❑ 35-45 ❑ 46-55 ❑ Over 55

10. How many hours per week do you read? __________

Name ____

Occupation ____

Address ____

City______________ State__________ Zip__________